DEADLY FLOWERS

A NINJA'S TALE

DEADLY FLOWERS

A NINJA'S TALE

SARAH L. THOMSON

BOYDS MILLS PRESS
AN IMPRINT OF HIGHLIGHTS
Honesdale, Pennsylvania

Thanks to Jodi Weinstein of the College of New Jersey
for her time and expert review.

Text copyright © 2016 by Sarah L. Thomson
Ornaments copyright © 2016 by Jim Carroll

Boyds Mills Press
An Imprint of Highlights
815 Church Street
Honesdale, Pennsylvania 18431

Printed in the United States of America
ISBN: 978-1-62979-214-9 (hc)
ISBN: 978-1-62979-563-8 (e-book)

Library of Congress Control Number: 2015953496

First edition
Production by Sue Cole
Design by Anahid Hamparian
The text of this book is set in Bembo.

10 9 8 7 6 5 4 3 2 1

*For Annie
and Liza*

O N E

I was sparring in the practice yard the day the new girl arrived.

Weak. She looked weak, and frail, and modest, and beautiful, and shocked at what she was seeing.

I blocked Masako's next blow easily—she was as slow as a water buffalo and not much less clumsy—and took a moment to glance around the yard.

Kazuko had just fallen off the pole she was trying to balance on. Aki had graduated to the tightrope and was walking serenely ten feet above our heads. Her sister, Okiko, was scaling a wall, with one of the older girls showing her how to place her feet. The little ones were leaping over bundles of hay, an instructor standing by to smack their bare toes with a bamboo rod if they touched the obstacle.

No one's toes were touching.

Two of the half-grown girls were trying to find Kiku in the grove of trees by the stream. They would have very little luck there, since she had hidden herself in the well. I hoped she wouldn't need to empty her bladder before the bell rang to mark the end of this training session.

If she stayed hidden, each of her pursuers would have to give her a portion of rice at dinner. If they found her, she'd have to do the same. Nothing like the prospect of kneeling hungry and watching half your meal disappear into somebody else's mouth to make you hide craftily or search inside every crack and under every stone.

Masako kicked. I dropped to one knee, seized her heel in one hand and her calf in the other, and flipped her over.

Then, like a fool, I glanced up to make sure the new girl was taking all of this in. If she were to stay, I wanted her to know who was the best in the practice yard.

In the moment when my gaze shifted, Masako surged up from the ground and tackled me, her arms around my waist. It was not an elegant move, but it was effective.

How many times had we been told? It doesn't matter *how* you get your enemy down—just get her down. And be sure she stays there.

I rolled us both in the dirt, grabbed Masako's hair with one hand, yanked her head back, and braced my forearm across her throat. Her eyes widened as her air was cut off, and an instructor's voice came from behind me.

"Kata, stop."

At the sound of his voice, I released the pressure on Masako's throat, and I heard her breath rush out as we both climbed to our feet. Our teacher tapped me on the shoulder, giving me the victory. Masako bowed her head, swallowed with a slight wince, and silently took her penalty for losing, a single stroke to her back from a thin, flexible strip of bamboo.

She kept quiet. If she'd cried out, it would have been two.

Silence is your greatest ally. Silence and darkness.

I waited, breathing deeply and slowly. If I'd panted out loud, there might have been a stroke with the bamboo rod for me, too.

The girl had come to a stop inside the gate, her hands to her mouth. Her kimono was as blue as the sea, embroidered with black and silver waves. Her hair, glossy with camellia oil, swung all the way down her back. Her face was horrified.

I stood there, barefoot, my hair spilling out of its braid, in my undyed, ragged jacket and trousers, covered in dust and straw and with a bit of blood trickling from my nose, and thought, *She won't last a week.*

TWO

Behind the girl, a man shut the gate that led to the road. He turned and strode past her. I looked him over quickly, in case I might have to serve him or fight him in the future.

He had loose trousers on beneath a short kimono that came only to his mid-thigh. So I knew he had been riding. He also had the two swords of a samurai, one long, one short, thrust through his sash, and a blue dragonfly embroidered on one shoulder. That meant he served one of the Kashihara brothers. Of course, so did most of the warriors for miles around.

When he paused to look back at the girl, I saw that he was missing half of his right ear. The scar ran down his neck and disappeared beneath his collar.

She caught his glance and hurried to catch up.

Obviously the girl was only here as long as the samurai was. It was foolish of me to have thought, even for a moment, that such a frail, frightened creature would be staying at the school. In any case, she seemed to be about my age, and fifteen was far too old to begin training. Most girls start when they are six or seven, young enough to cry for their mothers at night.

I had been even younger. And I'd been told that I never cried.

I watched the two of them leave their wooden sandals outside the door and enter without knocking. They were expected, then. The samurai must have had some errand with Madame Chiyome, and he'd brought the girl—his daughter, perhaps?—along. Why? Who could tell? Warlords and their warriors do not explain their reasons to the likes of us.

The bell rang for the end of practice. Kiku climbed triumphantly out of the well, and the girls raced inside. I lingered to let them all get ahead of me, and then followed, silently pleased. For some reason I felt satisfaction that the unknown girl had watched me win a bout, even with only clumsy Masako for an opponent. Even though the soft, pampered daughter of a rich man had nothing at all to do with me.

So I thought, until I found her that night, in one of the two upper rooms. She was standing with her straw sleeping mat rolled up in her hand, looking as wide-eyed as if a demon had snatched her out of her easy life and dropped her abruptly into the underworld.

"Well?" I said impatiently. "Put it down. Unroll it. You're staying the night?"

She nodded. Then she shook her head.

"You're *not* sleeping here? Then put the mat back. Someone else will need it."

She shook her head once more.

"You're staying for good?"

She didn't nod or shake her head or answer me in any way, and I threw out my hands in exasperation.

"Sleep standing up, then!" I snapped, and left her. She watched blankly as I walked through the room, making sure the four younger girls were settled for the night, kicking their mats straight, sliding the window screen shut to keep out ghosts and evil spirits, telling Aki and Okiko that I'd tie their thumbs into knots behind their backs if I heard them giggling, and ignoring Oichi whining that she was hungry. She would not have been if she hadn't wasted her time looking for Kiku in the trees. I blew out the flame of the lamp.

When I got back to my own mat, the girl had finally rolled hers out on the floor nearby. She undressed slowly, folding that gorgeous kimono tenderly and placing it in a cupboard. Then she curled herself up into a knot with her knees tucked in and her back to me.

At least she was quiet. Across the hall, someone wasn't. A miserable wailing rose and fell, like a cold wind sobbing with the voice of a hungry ghost. Little Ozu, probably. Masako should've kept her quiet. If Madame, downstairs in her own room, heard . . . Well, it would be better if Madame did not hear.

No one in my room made a sound. The girls knew I wouldn't allow any noise once the lamp was blown out.

I closed my eyes, blocked my ears to Ozu's crying, told my body to relax, counted backward from ten, and was asleep.

No dreams. I never allowed dreams to pursue me. Just rest, unbroken, until my eyes opened early in the morning, before the other girls were stirring.

But the next morning, the new girl was awake even earlier. She sat upright on her mat, hugging her knees and staring straight ahead.

We might have been close in age, but apart from that we could not have been more different. She was slender, with soft curves to her that were not muscle from hours and hours of sparring. Fair skin that had never sweated under the sun in the practice yard. Tender feet; she couldn't run barefoot over gravel or scale a stone wall with her toes. Soft hands with perfect nails and not a single callus from the hilt of a sword.

The younger girls were still sleeping, their soft breath filling the room. I sat up and winced. One of Masako's kicks had connected yesterday, and my shoulder was aching. I looked down and saw the spectacular purple bruise blossoming across my collarbone.

The new girl saw, too. She gasped.

"Please . . ." she whispered.

I looked over at her with an eyebrow raised as I gently rotated the shoulder to work the stiffness out.

Never ignore pain. Listen to it. But do not let it rule you. Pain is a messenger. Your mind is the general. The messenger tells you what is happening on the battlefield, but the general chooses the strategy.

"What *is* this place?" she begged.

She was terrified; I could see it. Like a horse about to bolt.

"Didn't anyone tell you?" I asked.

She shook her head. Her long hair, still sleek even after the night, spilled over her shoulders to brush the surface of her mat. I twisted my own hair, uncombed and dusty from yesterday, into a sloppy braid.

"It's a school," I said. "If you're staying, you're here to learn." Though surely she *wouldn't* be staying. Madame didn't take in girls like this, girls who'd never been hungry or cold or alone a day in their lives. Girls like this had other places to go. "*Are* you staying?" I asked.

"My uncle said . . ." She drew in a breath quick enough to make her shiver. "If I did as I was told, I could come home again. *Everything* I was told. What *kind* of school?"

But I had seen an idea begin to stir, there behind her eyes.

Fighting. Running and leaping and balancing. Climbing walls. Hiding in trees or down wells. She'd seen us at our training. What did she think all that was for?

I nodded.

The killer who slips through a crack in the window screen. The ghost no lock can keep out. The knife in the back. The garrote in the dark. The shadow with teeth as sharp as a wolf's.

"A school for girls. For flowers," I said as I felt a smile twist my mouth. "Deadly flowers. Ninjas."

And then I forgot about her.

Or I tried to. She was nothing to me, after all. Madame and the girl's uncle had some plan for her. Once the plan was carried out, she'd be gone. So why waste my thoughts on her?

But she was a puzzle. And my rebellious mind did not want to leave the puzzle alone.

I learned her name—Saiko. Did she have a family name as well? A girl like this might. She was clearly wealthy enough. But if she did, we never heard it.

Did that mean she was alone now, like the rest of us? Would she have to learn to live without a family behind her? That, even more than missing mothers and fathers and older sisters and aunties, was what sent some of the girls into sobbing fits at night. With no family to surround you, protect you, catch you if you stumbled, you might fall—and fall—and fall. You might never hit the ground.

You are alone. No one will come to your aid. You will survive on your own, or you will die.

Saiko, at least, did not weep at night. I never saw her sleep, though. She'd be awake on her mat when I closed my eyes, and in the morning when I opened them she'd be sitting up, looking out over the bodies of the sleeping girls.

"Sleep is a warrior's first duty," I said on her second night at the school.

Saiko looked over at me, startled.

"You keep your sword sharp," I reminded her. "You keep your bowstring dry. You have to keep your body ready and your mind alert, too. Sleep is the tool for that."

She stared at me as if I'd started babbling in the speech of the demons. I shrugged and lay down. In the morning she moved her mat away from mine.

Saiko spent no time in the practice yard. I never saw her with a weapon in her hand. But on the morning of her third day, I caught a glimpse of her inside the classroom, practicing with girls half her age how to walk across a bamboo floor without making a sound.

I was startled enough to stop at the doorway and stare. Saiko was wearing a simple dark-blue kimono and she held the skirts up to her knees, biting her lip with concentration as she gingerly set the edge of her right foot down, slowly rolling her weight onto the sole. A bamboo floor can squeak underfoot like a nest full of mice, but if you do the silent walk slowly enough, not a single noise will betray your movements.

One of our instructors was watching Saiko closely. We were never told our teachers' names; in my mind, I called this one Instructor Willow, for her slender frame and graceful arms. She'd only been at the school a few weeks, long enough for all of us to learn that she was quick with the bamboo rod.

Saiko learned it, too. The floor creaked, the strip of bamboo lashed down to smack the top of her foot, and tears welled up in her black eyes and spilled down her perfect, pale cheeks.

I moved on, before Instructor Willow could glance up and find me watching. Why was Saiko learning the silent walk? What use would it be to her?

Let nothing out of the ordinary escape your eye. Anything unusual is a warning, a clue, or a threat.

Saiko was no threat. But she *was* unusual. A weakling in a school for warriors, a rich man's daughter left with ninjas, who were lower in the minds of many than beggars or actors or the cleaners of corpses. Perhaps, if I kept an eye on her, I'd learn something about what Madame was planning. And since Madame controlled every single thing that took place in the school, down to which girl should be given the last mouthful of rice in the pot, it was always useful to know as much as possible about what was in her mind.

THREE

I did not see Saiko at all during that afternoon's training session. But then, I spent a fair portion of the session locked inside a cupboard, where it was hard to see much except my own knees.

Our other instructor, a hulk of a man I had privately named The Boulder, had tied my hands behind my back before shoving me into a cupboard that had been emptied of its bedding. He shut the door and latched it.

The cupboard was barely big enough to hold me. I was forced to crouch, my back hunched, breathing the smell of my own sweat.

"Get out of the school before I come back," The Boulder said, and I heard his footsteps moving away.

He'd given me no slack to work with. The cords around my wrists were tight. Of course they were. Did I think an enemy—if I were ever foolish enough to be caught—would do me the favor of binding my hands loosely?

But he had not stopped me from bunching up my hands into fists while he tied the knots. When I straightened my fingers and relaxed the muscles, there was the slightest give to the cords.

I pulled and pulled, straining my wrists apart. The bonds cut into my skin until I had to clench my teeth, but now I had more slack to work with.

Shoulder blades together, back arched, hands down—slowly, slowly, the loops tightening over my wrists, I pulled my bound hands past my hips and down along my thighs.

If I had no other choice, I could dislocate my shoulders to free my hands. I'd done it before. Once. It was something I'd save until the only other choice was death. Or failure.

Awkwardly, I wriggled myself into a sitting position, taking my weight off my feet. Then, with my hands tucked into the crooks of my knees, I stopped for a rest, trying to bend and stretch my fingers. I'd need them later. Not too long a rest, though. The Boulder would be back, and if he found me here, still bound and helpless, I would not like the consequences.

Plus I'd feel like such a fool.

My hands, now, must get past my feet. I'd already nudged my sandals off. The cords slid past one heel, then the arch of the foot, then the toes.

The second foot was easier.

There was light enough through the crack along the cupboard door that I could see the bonds around my wrists, now that my hands were in front of me. My own efforts had pulled the knots so tight that no amount of work with my teeth was going to loosen them. And the cords had sunk deep into my flesh.

My fingers were stiff. I suspected they were turning pale, although I could not see them well enough to be sure.

With difficulty, I tugged a wooden pin, about half the length of a chopstick, out of my hair. The enemy will take your sword, your knife, your lockpicks, but he will not bother with your hair ornaments.

All that my pin had for decoration was a round stone, halfway between brown and gray, polished smooth. It wasn't anything that would catch an admirer's eye, but then, it wasn't meant to. It had other uses.

My clumsy fingers fumbled with the thing and dropped it.

Ninjas should not curse out loud. Even a profane whisper can be heard just when you don't want it to be.

I did so anyway and picked up the pin awkwardly, gripping it between two fingers that were starting to go numb. Then I took the thicker end between my teeth and twisted the wooden stick to pull it in two.

Inside was a sharp sliver of a blade. I gripped the blunt end of the stick in my teeth and used the knife to cut the cords, then spent a few precious moments rubbing my aching, tingling hands and flexing my fingers, encouraging the blood to flow.

The cords had cut my skin in more than one place. I blotted the blood dry on my sleeves so I would not leave a trail.

And now the door. Simple. I screwed my hairpin back together and used the thin end to lift the latch that held the cupboard shut. Then I nudged the door open and checked.

The room, one of the two on the second floor of the house, was empty.

Snatching up my shoes, I slipped out of the cupboard and flipped the latch shut. Nothing to show that I was gone.

I reassembled the pin and slid it back into my hair. The cords that had bound me, I shoved in a pocket. They might be useful later.

Still barefoot, for the sake of silence, I went to the door. Kneeling low to the ground, I eased it open a slit and peered out. People naturally look at eye level when they are walking down a corridor. They are less likely to notice you if you are near the ground—or the ceiling.

Aki and Okiko were walking down the hallway, headed for the stairs. They, along with the other girls, would have been told to raise the alarm if they saw me. And my ability to get out of a locked cupboard would count for nothing if I could not also get out of the house.

I waited until the girls had disappeared down the staircase. Then I slipped through the door, sliding it shut behind me, and made my way out into the hall as quickly as I could while still moving quietly. I dared not take too much time. I had no idea when The Boulder would be back, no idea what he'd do when he found me gone. Instructors came and went at the school like leaves blown by the wind, hired by Madame for a month or two, maybe a week, now and then half a year. We never knew how long they would stay or what they did in the world beyond the school's gates. Madame wanted it that way. It ensured that we kept facing new, unknown opponents as we trained.

If it had been night, I could have gotten out of the building easily. This was the first time I'd been asked to do it in daylight. How was I going to hide when everyone could see me?

By getting to a place where no one would look.

There was a window to my right. I slid the screen open, then ducked down to the floor and waited while a maid passed by outside with a bucket of slops for the latrine. After she had gone, I gripped the cords of my sandals in my teeth, stepped up to the sill, turned so my back was to the yard outside, balanced, and took hold of the edge of the roof over my head.

Then a jump, pushing off with my toes, using my arms to lift myself up. I let my legs swing once to give me momentum, and I was on the roof.

I reached one leg down to slide the window screen shut with my toes. Not necessary, but elegant. The best ninja leaves no traces behind, blowing through an enemy's home like the wind. People say we can walk through walls. It's better if they keep on believing it.

A thatched roof isn't slippery, but it does make noise if you move quickly. And there are things living in it. With as much speed as I could manage while staying silent, I crawled up to the peak of the roof. Beetles scuttled across my bare feet and centipedes writhed over my fingers.

I clenched my teeth and shook one off my hand with a shudder. I hate centipedes. They have too many legs for any decent creature.

At the top I lay flat, so that I would not be silhouetted

against the sky. Cautiously I peered through the bristly thatch to be sure the coast was clear, then rolled so that I was on the other side. Here I faced only Madame's garden, where the girls and the servants were forbidden to walk, and beyond that the thick hedge that shielded the school from outside eyes.

I slid cautiously to the edge and dropped onto the roof of the classroom, only one story tall. From there I'd have an easier route to the ground. Then I heard a voice.

I had only heard that voice speak a few words in the last three days, but I still recognized it.

"Lift your arms. There. Knot the obi like this."

Curiosity is a good servant, but a bad master.

For that moment, I made a mistake and let curiosity rule me. I eased my head over the edge of the roof and peeked into the window below.

She was there—Saiko. She knelt at Masako's feet with her back to the window. Masako had on a silk kimono the color of the sun that was probably worth more than the house she stood in, with one end of her red obi tucked under her chin. She was trying to wind the rest of the silk belt around her waist, looking more alarmed than when, the day before, I'd swung a sharp blade straight at her head in the practice yard.

"But what if I tear it?" she was saying, indistinctly.

"You won't tear it if you walk the way I showed you," Saiko said firmly.

Intrigued, I let myself stay there, upside down in the window, my braided hair dangling down toward the ground.

Was this the answer to the riddle of Saiko? Was she here to teach girls how to wear a kimono or pluck their eyebrows or flirt behind a fan? Those were skills that might be useful; I could see that. An elegant kimono could be an effective disguise. But surely Saiko was not old enough to be an instructor, and no instructors ever revealed their names or slept beside the students at night. And why would someone here to teach the art of tying an obi need to learn the silent walk or be punished for letting a floorboard squeak?

"No, don't let it wrinkle," Saiko was telling Masako. "You'll look like a maid trying on her mistress's clothes. And leave your hair down!"

Fuku and Oichi, who knelt nearby, burst into laughter. If I'd been giving the lesson, I would have slapped them into attention.

"It's in my eyes. I can't see what I'm doing," Masako protested.

"I don't care. Never twist it up like that. Leave the back of your neck bare for anybody to see? It's shameless. Only a courtesan would do that. A very bold courtesan. Now, take a step. Go on. You won't trip."

Masako began to pace in a slow circle around the room, peering anxiously down at her feet. Fuku and Oichi were still giggling together. As Saiko turned to watch her student walk, she lifted her gaze and saw me. Or rather, my upside-down head framed by the window.

For a heartbeat we held each other's eyes. Then Saiko turned back to Masako as if she'd seen nothing more remarkable than a sparrow or a cloud crossing the sky.

"Mind your sleeves. Don't let them drag on the floor."

Careful to make no noise or sudden movement, I inched myself back up onto the roof.

Saiko had no reason to protect me. In a moment she'd call the alarm, and both instructors would be on my trail. Half of the girls, too. There were plenty who'd love to see me humiliated, not to mention whatever reward Madame would grant to the one who caught me. A bite of meat at dinner? A cake of sweet rice flour? Permission to sleep past dawn the next morning? Most of the girls would leap at the chance to earn a privilege like that.

"And stop looking at your toes! Fuku, will you be laughing when it's your turn?"

I let my breath out slowly. For the moment, at least, Saiko's lesson was continuing. She had spared me. I didn't know why. I didn't have time to wonder.

I sidled cautiously away from the open window, checked to see that Madame had not stepped outside for a stroll in her garden, and then gripped the edge of the roof so that I could flip over, dropping to the ground as quietly as I could. I ducked behind the bathhouse, took a moment to slide my straw sandals on and tie the cords around my ankles, and risked a dash along the curving garden paths.

Where two hedges met to make a corner, some hungry creature had gnawed through a root. I'd spotted the hole from the other side when, a few days ago, Instructor Willow had led us to the river for a test of how long we could swim underwater. At the time I'd thought it might make a good escape route, if I ever needed one. I needed one now.

Headfirst, I wiggled through the hedge, forced my way out—and flung myself into the soft dirt as the bright blade of a sword slashed down.

It wasn't a planned move, nor a graceful one. My instincts simply screamed, *Don't be here!* and I wasn't.

The blade snagged a strand of my hair as I rolled, and then I was up to face my attacker as quickly as I could, moving backward to put a pace or two between us. It was Instructor Willow. She must have known about the hole in the hedge, known that I had seen it. She'd been waiting here for me.

As I rolled, I'd snagged a handful of soft earth. Now, while the instructor recovered from her failed swing and drew back her blade for a thrust, I flicked the dirt into her face.

Several things happened next, very quickly.

Instructor Willow shut her eyes for a moment, and her thrust was slowed, so I could pivot out of range.

I snapped my arm forward, and my fist connected with her sword hand, right at the base of the thumb, where a cluster of nerves lies under the skin.

She gasped, and the sword fell. I knew how her arm must feel: limp and helpless, tingling from fingertips to shoulder.

I crouched low to snatch the sword and then swung around on one foot, the other leg extended. My straight leg hit her knees from behind and took her down onto her back.

The sword in my hand flashed for her throat. I saw her eyes widen.

"Stop."

My blade halted in the air, not two inches from my enemy's skin, the moment I heard Madame's voice.

Madame?

⁂

Sleep might be a warrior's first duty, but it wasn't coming easily that night.

I had two things to wonder about as I lay on my mat. The first was why Madame had come to watch a training exercise. The second was what, exactly, I'd been training for.

Not just escaping from a prison. I'd been doing that for years.

Something more. Something . . . important.

Did Madame think I had done well? Did she think I'd done well *enough*?

Could it be that she'd come to watch because she wanted to see if I was ready?

During the years I had lived with Madame, I'd seen it happen again and again. A girl, always older than myself, would simply vanish. Her mat would be empty one morning. There'd be nothing left but rumors that would flit among all the remaining students—Raku had infiltrated a samurai's castle, Haru had stolen a single jewel from a merchant's hoard, Toshi had died with a message undelivered, a failure, a disgrace to her training.

The girls who completed their missions didn't return. Students no longer, they were ninjas at last. There were always men with enough gold, eager to pay Madame for the skills and service of a deadly flower.

The girls who did not complete their missions . . . they didn't return either.

Now Masako and I were the two oldest ones left.

The air in the room seemed to prickle along my skin, as if a storm full of lightning were approaching. But I knew the sky outside was clear. It was my own anticipation that crackled like lightning.

What would my mission be? What would happen after it was over? Who would Madame sell me to? A warlord, a nobleman, a samurai, a criminal? What would it be like to put what I had learned to use in the service of a master?

I felt as if I were trying uselessly to peer into the depths of a black pit. I'd been at the school since I was three years old. There were only the smallest scraps of memory to tell me what my life had been like before Madame. I couldn't imagine what might happen to me without her.

But I was ready.

My first mission. I wouldn't be like Toshi. I would not fail. If only Madame thought so, too.

And perhaps she *wouldn't* think so, if she knew the truth—that I had *not* made it out of the house unnoticed. That I'd been seen. By Saiko.

I remembered Saiko's firm voice and clear instructions as she knelt at Masako's feet. She was not quite the timid little mouse I had thought her, at least not when it came to tying an obi. She'd surprised me then, and she'd surprised me a second time when she had lifted her eyes.

In that moment when our gazes had met, there had been some thought in her mind that I could not read.

If Masako had been the one to see me, she would not have called out the alarm. She would have felt pity for me, or for any girl being hunted, the same kind of pity she felt for homesick little Ozu. If it had been Fuku to catch me with my head in the window, she would have announced it gleefully and joined in the hunt. She had never liked me, and she was always hungry. An extra portion of rice at dinner would have been more than enough reward for her.

Saiko had not pitied me. Nor had she betrayed me. She had been thinking of something else as she went calmly on with her lesson.

I did not know what had been in her thoughts. But I knew that it made me feel uneasy to be in her debt.

FOUR

I was still wondering about Saiko the next morning, when I was called to Madame's room. I'd given the new girl half my millet porridge at breakfast, although she hadn't asked for it. I'd just slapped the bowl down in front of her without a word. It was my way to even the score between us, to show her that I no longer considered myself beholden to her.

The trouble was, I thought, as I slid open the door to Madame's room, that I did not know what Saiko might consider me to be.

"You performed well yesterday," Madame said after I'd entered and knelt to bow humbly and deeply. The mats beneath me were thicker and softer than those in the rest of the house, cushioning my knees.

Praise from Madame? The hairs on the back of my neck stirred uneasily, as if warning me that an attack must be coming. With her face as wrinkled as a rotten pear, her hair more white than black, Madame was no taller than Kazuko.

Masako towered over her and even I topped her by the breadth of a hand. But she was like a twisted silk cord that could fray to its heart without breaking. Every girl in the school had felt the strength of her hand on the bamboo rod. And she never offered words of approval.

"You have spent twelve years here," she went on in her thin voice, looking at me steadily as I knelt on the mat. "Time for you to prove you are worth all of your training."

In a flash, I jumped to my feet. I'd been right. Yesterday's assignment had been a test—and I'd passed.

"Oh, Madame—I will—I promise—thank you! I know I'm ready—"

She held up a hand.

Keep your face a mask. Betray your thoughts to no one.

I'd forgotten that rule entirely.

"Do you think I need you to tell me that you are ready? Do you think it is up to *you* to decide?"

Shamed, I gulped down the words in my throat and sank meekly back to my knees. I could only hope she would not decide I was no more than a child after all, and take the mission from my grasp.

"No, Madame," I murmured.

There was a tiny dish of pickled plums on the low table next to her. She picked up a slice delicately with her chopsticks and dropped it into her mouth. I waited while she chewed.

I was still hungry, having given away half my breakfast. I'd tasted a plum like that once. The smell of it, sharp and sour and still sweet, teased at my nose.

"There is a castle less than a day's journey from here," Madame said at last. "You'll enter it at night and make your way to a particular room. The person sleeping there is never to wake."

My throat tightened. My gut felt cold and heavy. Madame lifted another plum to her mouth.

I'd never heard of a girl whose first mission had been an assassination.

"It should not be difficult. You will have a confederate inside the castle. It will be her task to make sure the way to the room is clear for you to follow."

A confederate. I nodded dumbly, all the while wondering how I would complete the task. A blade? A tight cord across the windpipe? Poison? I knew so many ways . . .

Another plum.

"Your assistant will be Saiko."

"*Saiko!*" I blurted.

I would be going on my first mission with that weakling hanging around my neck? What did *Saiko* know of climbing a wall, wielding a sword, using a knife? What kind of mission could this be if *Saiko* were a part of it?

Madame's hand moved so quickly I could hardly see it. My head was snapped sideways by the force of her blow.

"You have some objection?" she asked, with perfect courtesy.

My left eye was watering, and the tears spilled down my burning cheek. I did not dare lift a hand to wipe them away.

"Speak, girl."

Madame never forgot the rules a ninja lived by. *Her* face was like the surface of a well; no one could guess what thoughts were hidden in the depths. I could not tell what she wanted now. A meek apology, or my true reasons for speaking as I had?

I took the risk, tightening my neck for the next blow, if it were coming.

"She's—she knows nothing, Madame," I said as steadily as I could. "She barely knows which end of a sword to hold! She could never—"

Her hand moved again. The blow was hard and fell in the same place as before.

"Are you proud of yourself, then?" Madame asked softly, her black eyes bright and merciless in their soft nests of wrinkled skin. "Do you think you know everything a ninja must know? Pah!" She nearly spat, as if her last slice of plum had been rotten. "You can scale a wall or swim a moat. No more than any foot soldier can do. Do you know the right moment to peer out from behind a fan? Can you catch a man's attention with one glance? Could you keep his eyes on your smile and off your hands?"

This time I knew she did not want me to reply. I kept my eyes on my knees.

"You sneer at Saiko? If I'd had her ten years ago, I could have turned her into a deadly flower every warlord in this land would fear. But that's not your concern. She has learned enough by now to do the task that is required of her. So have you. Get out. One of your instructors will give you all the details that you need."

I bowed again before I left the room, my cheek still stinging.

Now I knew what Saiko was doing here—learning just enough to help Madame's latest client dispose of someone he found inconvenient. And Madame, of course, had found a way to turn her temporary ninja to a bit of use in the few days she had spent at the school. It made sense.

But the satisfaction of having solved the puzzle of Saiko, and the thrill of my first mission, were soured by my humiliation.

Smiling and simpering and flirting behind a fan—were those skills a deadly flower needed?

Saiko, a ninja any warlord would fear? A better ninja than *me*?

◈ ◈ ◈

Could Saiko do *this*?

It had taken me about half a day to reach my destination, and now darkness, a ninja's dearest and closest ally, was wrapped tightly around me. The sky hid the moon behind thick clouds. My black trousers and jacket and the hood over my hair might have been made of the night.

Before me, a moat lapped gently at the shore. High above the black water, a bobbing light traveled like a spirit in the sky.

Some warlords preferred to live in the center of a town, with merchants and temples and pleasure quarters close at hand. The owner of the castle I was to infiltrate did not. His home was surrounded by farms and fields. A wooded ridge, too rocky and steep to plant, had offered me cover as I waited for the darkness to descend.

That darkness had been slow in coming. My imagination, with nothing better to do, began to wonder how many battles had been fought before those castle walls, how many soldiers had died here, and how many of their lost and hungry souls might be nearby. I whispered a quick mantra, holy words to protect me from the notice of a defeated samurai whose rage hadn't died with his body or a common soldier whose far-off family was too poor, too forgetful, or too dead to keep his spirit at peace with prayers and offerings.

Then I forced my attention back where it belonged. Even if there were ghosts nearby, they were not the greatest threat to my mission. And the light now moving above me was *not* a wandering soul, but merely a paper lantern in the hand of a guard walking the castle wall.

The light disappeared around a curve. I stayed where I was, huddled under the cover of a thick-leaved bush, and I counted steadily to seven hundred before it came back and vanished once again.

I had seven hundred seconds to make my way across.

Slowly, I slid into the water. No splash betrayed me. My sandals, tied together with a length of cord, hung over my shoulder, and in my hand was a short tube of bamboo. I swam underwater for as long as I could, then slipped a plug of wax out of one end of the tube and placed it to my lips before I eased up to just under the surface. Tugging the second plug out, I carefully let that end of the tube up into the air and drew in enough breath to continue before swimming on. Two more breaths, and my fingers touched a rough block of stone.

I'd counted to five hundred, so I stayed there, under-water, my breathing tube just breaking the surface, and went on with my numbers. Above me, I knew, the guard's lantern light was going past.

When I reached seven hundred, I tucked the tube away inside my jacket and surfaced, shaking water from my eyes.

Perhaps I'd counted a bit quickly, or perhaps the guard had moved more slowly this time. The light was just above me, spilling a slick yellow glow down the wall.

But he could not see me clinging to the stones, unless he stuck his head over to peer out. And why should he do that? I'd made no noise. He had no reason to suspect I was here.

The light moved along the wall and was gone once more.

Down here, near the water, the wall was at its broadest, narrowing toward the top. That made the climb simple, and so did the cracks between the stones, wide enough for my fingers and toes.

My first mission, and it was *easy*. I could have laughed, if I'd dared risk the noise.

When I got perhaps halfway up, the slope vanished. The wall now rose straight above me, and I'd run out of handholds. The stones were set closer here, and the cracks were too narrow to wedge my fingers into.

Inside a pocket of my jacket I had half a dozen iron stakes, narrow but strong. Each had one end that had been hammered flat, and one that was blunt and thick.

Working silently, I wedged the flat end of one stake between two stones. Standing on it, I balanced and placed the next at waist height.

It was slow and tedious climbing, since I had to reach down with my toes to pull each stake out as I advanced. I could have left them, to be a ladder down when I returned, but I might need to climb another wall, inside. And there was no hurry, after all. It was only the hour of the rat; the night was still my friend.

The last time the guard passed by above me, I was so close that I could have reached up and tapped his ankle. I smiled as I held my breath, balanced motionless on my stakes, a black spider on a stone wall.

Suppose I actually did it? He'd look down. He'd gasp. He'd drop the lantern and it would skid down the wall to splash in the moat, its flame drowned in an instant.

Then we'd be in darkness, and the darkness would be on my side.

Would I slide down the wall and out of his sight, leaving him to think a ghost had plagued him?

Would I scramble up and plant a kiss on his cheek before I slid down the interior wall to safety?

Would I yank his feet out from under him and send him crashing down to drown in the moat?

Would I kill him?

Kill some poor soldier whose only fault had been to walk along a wall? No reason why I should not. I was on a mission to kill. I'd been training all my life. I knew more ways than I could count to end a life.

But I had never actually *done* it. I'd never killed any-thing larger than a wriggling trout for dinner.

Of course I didn't reach up and tap the guard's leg as he passed above me. What ninja would imperil her mission like that? Instead I clung motionless to the wall, and his footsteps slowly faded away above me.

Then I heaved myself up and over the edge.

FIVE

Getting down the other side of the castle wall was easier. Some careless person had allowed a beech tree to grow too close. It was just a quick jump to a thick branch, with no more noise (I hoped) than a squirrel would make. Barefoot, I shimmied along the smooth bark of that branch to reach the trunk, and from there it did not take long to scramble down and put my sandals back on.

Next I got lost in a garden.

Oh, I was sure this warlord's gardens were beautiful by day. The winding paths no doubt made a pretty pattern when viewed from the windows of his mansion, high on its hill. His guests must have appreciated the artistically arranged boulders that blocked my path. They probably enjoyed strolling across the graceful bridges that I did not dare use and wrote poetry about the shallow pools that I was forced to pick my way through. I also imagined the warlord laughing at the idea of a stranger trying to find her way through his grounds without a guide.

I knew the warlord's home would be at the highest point, so in the end I simply headed uphill, climbing over anything that lay in my way. It meant I left more trampled grasses and broken twigs than I would have liked, but the hour of the rat was slipping past, and the hour of the ox was approaching. I could not wander in this maze until dawn.

Finally I broke free of the trees, and I could see the cluster of buildings where the warlord and his retainers dwelled—the barracks for his samurai, the stables for his horses, the towering stone keep where he could retreat if danger threatened, and the comfortable mansion for when he felt secure.

Most of the mansion's windows and all of its doors were shuttered, but here and there lamplight still glowed through rice paper screens. A tiled roof swooped gracefully and conveniently low over the pale white squares. I watched long enough to be sure no guards were on duty. Then I slipped my sandals off once more, ran, leaped, and was up on the roof. My next task was to find an open window.

It was where Instructor Willow had told me to look. She had given me all the details of my mission, as calmly as if I hadn't been two inches from cutting her throat the day before. Now I headed for the building's northeast corner, lowered myself from the roof, and slipped inside. I stood at one end of a long corridor. To my left was a wall made of paper screens from floor to ceiling; behind those screens were rooms where the occupants of the mansion were sleeping. To my right was a wall made up of tall wooden shutters, covering windows like the one I had just entered through.

I slid the shutter of that window closed and stood still for a moment to listen.

Deep breathing. Someone snoring. A dog barked outside. Were there more four-footed guardians inside? I didn't think so. I could hear no claws clicking on bamboo floors.

I did hear someone whistling softly, far away. Halfway down the corridor, a light was glowing dimly through rice paper. Not everyone in this house was asleep. At any moment, someone might open a screen and step out into a corridor. A soldier might be on patrol. A servant might be hurrying to finish an errand. A guest might be too restless to doze.

I had never—*never*—realized how this would feel. I had trained for this, yes. I'd imagined it, certainly. I'd been waiting for my own mission for years.

But I'd never known how it would actually feel to be alone in a house full of people who would kill me if they found me.

It felt *wonderful.*

My veins were humming with the rush of my blood; my skin tingled. Once, at the school, I had woken up to find a tiny mouse nibbling at the straw of my sleeping mat. I'd trapped it with one hand, and felt its heart thrumming against my palm. My heart seemed to be beating almost that fast now.

I could float or fly. I could walk through walls. I could tie a knot in a cat's tail, steal both a samurai's swords, trim the warlord's mustache while he slept.

The dark and sleeping world was my playground. And at playtime's end—

A knife. Hot blood on my hands. Death, quick and cold and silent.

I felt my heartbeat slowing. Which was good, no doubt. No doubt. I was not here to play, and overconfidence is a ninja's worst enemy, even more so than the moon.

I felt delicately with my bare feet along the smooth floor.

A hard, dry grain of rice under my toes. Another. I walked forward carefully, not letting a single slat of bamboo creak under my weight, and passed the lighted window so silently that I could hear a brush whispering over paper inside the room. The rice guided me onward, telling me where to go at each turn in the corridor.

The trail led me to a corner around which came a soft yellow glow of light. I knelt, keeping my head near the floor, and took a cautious look.

My body stayed rigid, but my heart jerked inside me like a fish on a hook.

What was *she* doing here?

I got to my feet and edged silently around the corner, making no sound, none at all. But the elegant figure in the pale green kimono, holding a small oil lamp carefully in her hands, turned and bowed humbly to me.

She could not be humble enough for my liking. What did Saiko think she was doing?

She had been told to leave the window open and drop the rice for me to follow. And no more! This was *my* mission. She would ruin everything.

I quickened my pace a bit, but still walked carefully—I could not risk a tattletale floorboard now. The trail of rice ended at the door where Saiko stood.

Never let anger make you careless. Anger can be your weapon, or it can be your death.

"Go. Away," I growled under my breath as I reached Saiko's side.

She bowed again. But she didn't speak. And she didn't leave.

I gestured furiously that she should go.

She stayed.

You'll get us killed! You don't know how to do this! I howled. Silently. In my mind.

I realized, with a small, sharp shock, that there was nothing I could do to make her leave if she did not want to go. Should I shout at her? Hit her? Simply invite the warlord and his guards to arrive at a run?

I glared and reached out to pinch the wick of her lamp between my fingers. If she *had* to contaminate my mission with her presence, she could at least refrain from announcing to the sleeping household that we were here.

Darkness swooped in on us, soft and reassuring. I reached out to brush my fingers over the door, feeling for the edge where the paper screen joined the frame. I drew a knife from my sleeve and cut the screen neatly, keeping the slit as invisible as possible. Then I reached inside and lifted the latch.

The door was well made. It slid noiselessly open.

I stepped in, Saiko on my heels. Better than having her

in the corridor, I supposed. At least she held the skirt of her kimono carefully in one hand, so that it didn't rustle.

I slid the door shut behind us. Then I stood still and waited.

The breath of a sleeper rose and fell, somewhere in the room. It was deep and steady, but not too steady. Little hesitations and deeper sighs now and then told me that the room's inhabitant was truly asleep, not pretending.

Slowly, slowly, the darkness opened up to let my eyes in.

A chest with something draped casually over it—a kimono, no doubt. A window in the far wall. A futon on the floor, with a shape huddled there.

The shape of—who?

I did not know. Knowing who my knife would slide into was not part of my mission.

Some drunken lord, a commander of soldiers, sleeping off his rice wine? Some fat merchant, snorting in his bed? Some young samurai, barely old enough to wear his swords?

Someone who knew something he should not. Someone who had offended with a careless look or word. Someone whose life had become inconvenient to a man, or perhaps a woman, with enough gold to pay Madame for my time and my skills and my quickness with a blade. A garrote would have been quieter, but a blade was quicker. And I was not sure I could bear to let this take long.

I eased toward the shape on the bed, my feet slower than ever. There was no rush now, and everything depended on silence.

Saiko was behind me. She was silent, too; her few days of training must have done her at least a bit of good. Her presence, so close, felt like having a ghost hover at my shoulder. I could not even hear her breathing. I only knew she was there from the stir of air at the back of my neck.

I wanted to kill her much more than I wanted to kill the stranger on the bed.

My feet glided, brought me closer, closer. I felt I was swimming through air, or slipping into black water as warm as my blood. Perhaps I, not Saiko, was the one who had become a ghost.

I slid gently to my knees beside the futon. The sleeper turned. The mattress did not rustle under him, as straw would; it must have been stuffed with wool or cotton. The silk quilt sighed. I waited, motionless. No breath. I would have stopped my heart from beating if I could. I held my knife low. It waited patiently in my hand, the blade blackened with a mixture of soot and grease.

It was the moon that betrayed me.

A cloud must have slipped away from its light, because the window in the far wall brightened.

Everything in the room took on a sharper focus. I could see a pattern, like ripples in water, sewn into the kimono that lay across the chest. I could see the weave of the mats on the floor.

I could see the sleeper's face.

A boy. He was no more than a boy.

There was time. It would only have taken a moment or two. I could have covered that sleeping face with a pillow;

I could have thrust the knife home.

I did not. He could not have been older than ten. How could a child be a danger to anyone? Who could he have offended? What did he know that he should not?

The moon had betrayed me. I betrayed my training. I hesitated. My hand did not tremble, but my knife did not move.

And Saiko made a sound.

It was something between a gasp and a sob. I turned, angrily. Her hand was at her mouth.

I looked back, and the boy was awake.

He sat up, the quilt falling from his shoulders. His eyes and his mouth were wide in his moonlit face. He was frightened enough by the sight of me, a dark figure with a blade in her hand, but his real astonishment was for Saiko.

"Older sister?" he whispered.

SIX

I should have killed him. I should have killed them *both*.

Instead, I stood there with my knife in my hand, its blade cutting nothing worse than air, and stared dumbly as Saiko took command.

Command of *my* mission!

"Silence," she whispered, and dropped to her knees beside the futon. I might as well have been a pillow on the floor for all the attention either one of them paid me. "He's planning to kill you, Ichiro. You must come with us."

I had a knife, I had a sword, I had a cord for a garrote; I had half a dozen ways to end this. But I could not make myself use any of them.

Had Saiko planned this? Had she *known*?

And what was that boy, Ichiro, doing? He'd thrown the quilts aside and squirmed off the futon, digging a hand underneath, as if he were looking for something. How long before someone—a servant, a guard, a late-night reveler—walked down the corridor outside, heard voices or sounds from this room, and decided to investigate? How long before every armed man in this mansion was hunting us down?

I'd failed. My knife was clean of blood. And I didn't have it in me to stab the boy while he knelt with his back to me, as if he'd never dreamed I could be a threat.

Saiko would have stopped me, in any case. Shouted. Screamed. Unless I killed her, too. And there was no time, no time . . .

Could I get the pair of them back through the corridor and to the window I'd used to enter the house? Almost no chance. The boy didn't know the silent walk, and I doubted that Saiko could keep it up for the length of one corridor, much less several. The bamboo floor would betray us. And neither of them knew how to hide—or, if we were discovered, how to kill.

But there was another window, here in this very room. Minutes later the three of us were scrambling out of it.

I swung myself up to the roof, two stories above the ground, and then lay flat, stretching out my hand to the boy. He took it and got himself up without too much effort, his bare feet giving him purchase on the slippery tiles.

Saiko's kimono dragged at her when she tried to follow; the thing weighed more than a heavy child. I groaned silently, gripped her wrists, and tried to haul her up by my own strength. The boy wiggled closer to grab at the shoulder of her kimono and help as best he could.

Between the three of us, we managed it at last, but we

slipped and slid on the tiles of the roof, and the operation was not quiet. A latch lifted below us and a window screen slid open. "Who's there?" asked a voice, slurred with sleep and rice wine.

We stayed frozen on the roof, listening. Seconds slid by, slow as blood seeping through a bandage. If we were seen . . .

Well, I could run. But the two of them? Never. I'd have to leave them behind, and my mission would be more of a failure than it already was.

The voice grunted and the window slid shut.

I lifted a hand in warning. We held still while I counted slowly to fifty. Then I drew my knife from my belt.

I heard the faintest gasp in the darkness before I sliced through Saiko's obi and yanked the heavy green silk off her back. Her under-robe was plain, and the silk was much lighter; hopefully it would not weigh her down. We left her outer kimono in a crumpled heap, with her socks on top. Bare feet would keep her from slipping. I hoped.

I didn't like it, leaving belongings behind, like a banner announcing the way we'd gone. But we had no choice. I beckoned, and we fled.

Oh, the two of them were *slow*. And loud. It was like dragging two enormous boulders behind me. But we managed to get across the roof, to the northeast corner, where we'd have the shortest distance to cover before we were once more in the trees.

I swung myself to the ground, and Saiko followed. The boy hesitated. We didn't have time for hesitation. I gestured angrily at him to come down.

He slid over the edge awkwardly, dangling from one hand. Little Ozu would have done it better. Then his fingers slipped, and he fell.

I shoved Saiko aside and caught him in midair. He wasn't that heavy, but enough to knock us both sprawling in the soft dirt. At least he knew enough not to make a sound.

Even so, I clamped a hand over his mouth and waited until I could be sure his incompetence had attracted no attention. Then I pushed him off and rose to my feet. Crouching, we made it to the tall grass, and then into the trees. Under the shelter of their branches I drew in my first full breath in what seemed like years.

If I'd only had myself to worry about, I could simply have run downhill until I met the wall, climbed it, and vanished into the dark. But there was no hope that Saiko and the boy would be able to scale a wall. We'd need that beech tree.

I just had to *find* the cursed thing.

I crawled through bushes, skirted ponds, dodged boulders, paused and backtracked and walked in circles, Saiko and the boy stumbling at my heels. And I found nothing, *nothing*, that looked familiar.

The sun would come up and the three of us would still be wandering here. *Oh, Lord Whoever-You-Are, we were admiring the elegant bridge over this pond, the one that idiot boy just stumbled into up to his knees . . .*

The idiot boy, standing stupefied in the water, made

a choked, gulping sound, as if something was stuck in his throat.

When I turned to tell him to keep his mouth shut, I saw what he was looking at.

Her kimono was white. Her face was white, too, and she seemed to glimmer against a stand of smoky dark cypress, as if she'd been shaped out of cloud and would soon drift apart and blow away.

At first I knew she would scream, and we would be lost. Then I knew she was a ghost, and we were worse than lost—we were cursed.

But when she walked a few steps toward us, I saw her feet in sandals and neat white socks just under the skirt of her kimono. Then I knew she was no ghost. But I didn't trust that she was human either.

I'd never seen a face like hers. Saiko was beautiful, but next to this woman, she looked as plain as—well, as plain as me.

Her eyes were narrow and elegant and black. Her eyebrows lifted over them like graceful wings, and they made her whole face seem light and daring, as if at any moment she could dart away into the sky. Her red lips opened, and her teeth were even as a row of pearls. Why had I expected them to be filed to sharp points, like a hungry animal's?

It did not occur to me, then, to wonder how I could see so many details of her face, there in the dark of the garden, away from any fire or lantern.

My sword was in my hand, as if her beauty were something to fight. But she did not step back or put up her hands for mercy. She only stretched out one arm and pointed. The long sleeve of her kimono swung like a white wave in the black air.

"That way," she said simply. Her voice was not what I had expected—low and warm and somehow rough, as though she might have growled as easily as she had spoken. Once the words left her mouth, she stepped between two tree trunks, and in a moment she was gone.

Saiko started to move in the direction the woman had pointed. The boy sloshed to the edge of the pool and climbed out.

"Wait!" I whispered.

"She said this way." Saiko glanced back at me.

"And you *believed* her?" Why should we obey directions from a mysterious woman in white, haunting a nighttime garden? Why would she help us? Why should we trust her?

Saiko's voice was calm, but she shrugged my hand off her arm. "You're lost. And we must go some way. This is as good as any other."

Then we heard the noise.

I didn't know if someone had seen the cut I'd left in the door screen and checked the boy's room, or if someone had found Saiko's kimono on the roof, or if the woman in white had set pursuers on us. All I knew was that, from uphill, voices shouted. And I glimpsed lantern light bobbing between the trees.

The hunt was on.

Ninjas should not curse. I cursed. Then I dropped to my knees, and dug inside my pockets. The fickle moon was my ally for the moment, giving enough light that I could see what to do. Later on it might betray us all.

"Go," I whispered at Saiko. "Look for a beech tree by the wall, and wait there. I'll find you."

She went, the boy following, in the direction the woman in white had told us.

Small wooden boxes, five of them, strung on a waxed cord—my fingers found them, and I pulled them out and laid them in the soft grass, stretching the cord between each one to its full length.

Everything was damp from my swim through the moat. But not so damp that this would not work.

I hoped.

I fished another box from inside my jacket. My fingers slid over the slick surface and found the catch. Lacquer and wax on the outside of the box had kept water from the chunk of flint and piece of steel inside.

I took the knife from my sleeve and quickly frayed one end of the cord. The soft heart of the silk was still dry enough to catch the spark that leapt onto it when I struck my flint with my steel.

I waited while the spark grew into a tiny flame, even as the voices uphill grew louder. Then I ran after Saiko and the boy.

They were at the base of the tree. So the stranger in the white kimono had been trustworthy after all—so far, at least. I'd caught up to them when the first of my gunpowder boxes exploded.

The boy nearly jumped out of his skin. I had no time

to explain. "Follow!" I ordered, and was up the tree before he'd turned to stare.

As my second box exploded, I leaned down to grab the boy's hand and pull him up. We made it to the fork in the tree where the branch stretched out toward the wall, about two stories above the ground, and waited while Saiko struggled up below. She made the tree shake as if a bear were climbing it. But the noise and confusion in the garden below would hide a great deal. With luck we'd be over the wall and away before anyone inside the castle realized they'd been tricked.

Luck had been lacking from this mission for some time, however.

"I'll go first," I murmured. "Then you." I touched the boy's arm. "Saiko, you last. Lie flat on this branch and crawl for as long as you can stay on it. Then swing from your hands. I'll help as much as I can. Saiko, make sure he's on the wall before you start. The branch won't hold two."

"I don't know if I can hold on," the boy said humbly.

Those were his first words to me. He sounded ashamed, as if he hated to be causing trouble, but just couldn't help it.

"Haven't you ever climbed a tree before?" I asked impatiently.

The boy held out his right hand. The palm was black with blood in the moonlight, and a gash was still oozing.

"I cut it on a broken tile on the roof. I'm sorry," he said.

It was a bad cut, and he hadn't made a sound at the time. I began to have a glimmer of respect for him, even as I wondered if he'd left a trail of blood all over that roof.

Was that how our pursuers had tracked us? Right now was not the moment to wonder about it. Right now I had to get the boy over to the wall.

I was already untying the wide cotton belt around my waist as the third explosion cracked the night open, and the yelling in the garden below doubled in volume. My belt was more than a belt, actually—wide enough to be a cloak or a hood, strong enough to tie up an enemy, long enough to help me climb a wall or mount a roof.

I tied the cloth quickly around the boy's chest, just under his arms, and slipped the loop on the free end over my wrist.

"Lie flat on the branch, and *don't move* until I'm across," I instructed in a low voice. "When I'm on the wall, crawl out as far as you can go. When you can't crawl any more, slide off. I'll pull you up. Use your hands and feet to help me. Understand?" He nodded. His eyes were wide, his face solemn. He was frightened. Good. A frightened boy would listen. He would follow my commands.

I made it across, twisted the cloth loose from my wrist, and gripped it tightly in both hands. Then I knelt, so the boy's weight would not (I hoped) pull me off balance.

He crept out along the tree limb. Cautiously. Too cautiously. How much time did we have? I didn't know. I could only hope every guard along the wall had run to investigate the sound of my gunpowder boxes exploding. If they had not, we were all dead.

The boy tried to crawl a little quicker. But when the branch began to wobble under him, he slowed again.

I saw him slip, tightened my grip, and braced myself for his weight. He swung from the tree and toward the wall. *Please, let no one be watching from below . . .*

He had the sense to use his feet to break the force of his impact against the wall, but still he hung breathless for a few moments while I began to haul him up.

It was not easy. He helped as much as he could, but the injured hand made him clumsy.

Saiko began to creep out along the tree branch. Hopefully, she could manage for herself. Dragging one person up this wall was work enough.

The fourth box exploded. The boy was closer. I hauled again, wedged the slack cloth under my knee, got a fresh grip.

His left hand appeared over the edge. I grabbed it with my right, leaned over, and looked down into the boy's relieved smile.

The smile melted into a look of horror.

His hand was slick with sweat, as was mine. My grip was slipping.

Frantically the boy kicked and dug at the wall with his toes, making himself swing. I hissed at him to be still, or he'd have us both over.

At that moment, I could have let his hand slide free. I could have let him go. This wall was higher than a house; he would not have been likely to survive the fall.

My belt was still tied around his chest, but I did not have to grab the free end. I could have claimed to Saiko that it had been an accident, that he'd been gone before I could save him.

It was what I'd been sent to do. It was what I'd been trained to do. And I never once thought of doing it.

As his left hand slid farther through mine, the boy scrabbled at his neck with his right. Was he choking? On what? Why *now*?

He pulled something over his head and thrust it at me. "Take it!" he gasped, terrified.

"Get my other hand!" I was flat on the wall now, reaching for him with my left hand while clinging as hard as I could with my right.

"Take it!" It was a whisper and a scream, and as I got a grip on his free hand I felt something between our palms, something small and round and hard.

Then I heaved with all the strength in both my arms, and he was on top of the wall. Saiko landed beside us, dropping to her knees to grab at the boy's shoulders. He was quivering like a rabbit. I heard him bite back a sob.

She could deal with him now. It was entirely her fault that he was here at all.

SEVEN

On the top of the castle wall, I shoved whatever the boy had given me into a pocket so I could have both hands free to tie knots in my belt, one every two feet. I heard my fifth and last gunpowder box blow, drove one of my iron stakes into a crack between two stones, and dropped the loop of the belt over it.

"Slide down. Go," I whispered.

Saiko peered into the watery blackness. "I can't swim."

Of course she couldn't. "Can you?" I demanded of the boy.

He nodded.

"Then you go down first. Swim for the opposite side. Saiko, you climb down next and wait till I come. Hold onto the belt. I'll get you across." If I didn't leave her to drown as she richly deserved for turning my simple mission into this—I didn't even have a word for it, what the three of us were in the middle of. This—this *mess*.

The boy went over. I didn't hear the splash. But I did feel the rope go slack.

Then Saiko.

And then me.

The water of the moat felt cool on the aching muscles in my arms. I whispered to Saiko to float on her back. She had both hands still locked around my dangling belt, and she didn't obey. I could feel her shaking.

"Drowning is a better death than being hit by an arrow," I growled at her. "Let *go!*"

With a gasp, she did so, and I pulled her onto her back and set out to drag her across with me. She gripped my forearm, across her chest, with both hands as tightly as a samurai grips his sword. She was terrified.

Well, she deserved to be. She should be peacefully asleep on a soft futon inside the castle at this moment. She was *supposed* to be there. She was not supposed to be clinging to my arm, slowing down my escape.

And the boy . . . the boy was supposed to be dead.

"It's all right," I gasped, and spat out a mouthful of water and scum. "I won't let you drown."

I wouldn't swear not to strangle her once we reached the shore. But I supposed I could promise not to let the water have her. We'd gotten to the other side of the moat when a soldier found my belt hanging from the wall.

One day some genius of a ninja will invent a rope that unknots itself and comes when you call it, one that you don't have to leave hanging behind to announce how and where you escaped.

The guards would never have spotted me, all in black, like my ally the night. But Saiko was in white silk, and the boy in undyed cotton. Arrows came humming through the air like maddened bees. All we could do was run.

They would not follow us down the wall; soldiers were trained for fighting, not for climbing. Not in full armor, certainly, and carrying weapons and shields to weigh them down. They'd have to run along the wall to the stairs and then find a gate. We had a few minutes.

Maybe two.

At least one.

We headed uphill, for the forest where I had watched the sun go down. Fortunately, I hadn't been idle while I was waiting.

"Get in!" I gasped, sliding to my knees beside the muddy hole I'd dug under the shelter of a little overhang along a small ridge of rock. The boy understood, and slithered in. Saiko gave a gasp of horror. I knew what she was thinking. Dirt, spiders, centipedes, worms . . .

I shoved her in, piled dead leaves and branches over both of them, and leaped for a limb of the pine tree overhead.

I had only dug one hole. I hadn't thought I'd need to hide anyone but myself.

One last effort from my tired arms, and I was up. But not high enough. There was another, wider branch above me that I had my eye on. I made it just before the first of the soldiers burst into the wood.

I lay flat and still, pressing my face against the tree's

rough bark. The living sap inside the wood sent back a faint echo of my heartbeat.

This is how to stay invisible: Be where no one will look.

When people are searching a wood at night, they look behind trees. They poke spears into bushes. They shout "There you are!" to startle their quarry into movement.

But they do not expect their prey to turn into a badger or a mole, and burrow into the earth. Or into an owl, taking refuge among branches and leaves. They rarely look down. And they rarely look up.

Rarely, of course, does not mean *never*.

One of the soldiers stopped beneath my tree.

Once, when I was younger, I'd held my breath when I was hiding, until I could not hold it anymore. My gasp for air led the instructor right to me. I remembered the *crack* of bamboo across my shoulders.

So I did not hold my breath now. I let it ease out slowly between my lips. Moving air in the nose may squeak or hum. Moving air in the mouth is silent.

I welded myself to the branch. It was broad enough to stay steady beneath me.

He could not have heard me. He could not have seen me.

But he didn't *go*.

I stared down at his helmet. His shoulders. The dark lumpish shape of him in the shadow.

Why wouldn't he just *go*?

I still had my sword. But this was a man, bigger than I was, older and stronger, too. Most probably a soldier who had survived many a battlefield. Which meant that he was used to killing enemies.

And I was not.

Still, if I leaped down, I'd surprise him. That might allow me to kill him. It would not, however, allow me to kill his companions if they heard the two of us fighting for our lives.

If he looked up, I'd have to do it.

Should I do it *before* he looked up?

It would make noise. I couldn't risk it.

If he looked up and saw me, then *he'd* make noise.

No reason he should look up. No reason he should stand there, either. But he was doing it.

Go away, I thought fiercely. *Go away, go away, go away.*

He didn't seem to be listening.

I'd count to one hundred. If he didn't move before then, I'd do it. I'd jump.

But, oh, how I wished for something—a rustle in the undergrowth, an owl's ghostly call, a glimmer of moonlight on a shaking leaf—to catch his attention before I was done counting.

Eighty-eight, eighty-nine, ninety . . .

Something snorted and scrambled in a thicket, not twenty yards off. My soldier's head came up.

Would he really go? Yes, he would. Whatever had moved in the bushes—badger, bear, mole?—had been enough to keep his attention. He followed the sound, sword out, and then he was lost in the darkness.

A shiver took hold of me from the inside, shaking me as

a dog does a rat. How had it gotten so cold? I commanded my muscles into stillness. I wasn't safe yet.

The noise of the searching men gradually died away. I did not move. The smaller sounds of the night came back, the sweet rasping of the crickets, the dashes and scurryings of little hunted things.

Then, finally, I slid down, stiff and sore and clumsy from lying so long without moving. I made my way to the hole I'd dug and pulled off the branches and brush.

"Time to go," I said to the two filthy faces looking up at me.

※ ※ ※

I hauled them out of their burrow and dragged them as far as I dared, cutting off every attempt at talk. At all costs, we must be as far away from the castle as possible before daybreak. Briefly I even risked the dark, deserted main road, and the risk paid off; we met no one.

But they were both clumsy and slow, caked with mud (which at least made them harder to spot in the darkness), and stupid with tiredness. The night had worn me down as well. My first mission, my very first, and it had turned into this.

After the boy had fallen twice, and needed my help to get up the second time, I led them both off the road and up into the trees. A little clearing gave us a stretch of flat grass. We all sank down, panting.

A ninja out of legend would have stayed awake for what was left of the night to watch for pursuit. A ninja out of legend could go for days without rest or food.

There were no legends here. If I didn't give myself a few hours of sleep, I'd never get us all home.

Home?

That was a strange word to drift into my head as I stretched out on the hard ground next to Saiko and her little brother, feeling my tense muscles ease one by one. I had scraps and tatters of memory connected with the word *home*, and they were not of the school. A dark farmhouse with a single room. Sleeping snug between a brother and a sister, on the floor beside the hearth. The smells of sweat and dirt, wood smoke and warmth.

But that had been long ago.

Now I had the school, and Madame—no. That was wrong.

Cold fear drenched me like water from a bucket, sending shivers from my scalp to my toes.

I didn't have the school any longer. Madame had trusted me with my first mission, and I'd failed. More than that—I'd failed *and* survived.

That was not supposed to happen.

No girl came back to the school after her first mission. If she lived, she was sold. If she died, she was dead.

But where else could I go?

I had no family, no village, no lord. No one to take me in. I could not simply . . . run. No one ever did.

The school was harsh, the training difficult, but no student ever tried to escape. We all knew that the world around us held no place for orphan girls who were not pretty enough to be courtesans, humble enough to be nuns, or rich enough to be wives.

Running away would mean being not just alone but adrift. Forever.

I had been both of those things once, when *home* had vanished, washed from the earth like ink from a wet stone. Not again. Never again. The school was a hard place, but I had made it into *my* place. Somewhere to belong.

I would have to return. I'd have to take Saiko with me.

And the boy, still inconveniently alive? Perhaps there was something that could be done about that . . .

I laid my sword beside me, the blade bare on the grass, where I could snatch it up in an instant if I needed it. Then I curled up and slept alongside Saiko and the boy, dreamless as usual, until someone giggled very close to my ear.

My hand was reaching for my sword before my eyes had opened, but then I paused.

Something else was interested in my sword as well.

I lay on my side with my face half in the grass, and the little creature was just tall enough to look me in the eye. In the cool gray light before dawn, I could see that it was black and feathered, with a sharp, curved beak. But its eyes, peering craftily at me over the hilt of my blade—its eyes were human.

Clearly I was dreaming.

Ghosts riding the night air, monsters lurking in mountain passes, demons huddled in the darkest shadows—any sensible person understood where they might be and wore a charm or knew a mantra to keep them at bay. But no one ever expected to *see* one.

A tengu, looking in my eye? A tengu studying my sword? A tengu making a very rude gesture with the clawed finger on the end of one feathered wing?

It couldn't be. My eyes were muddled by sleep. I blinked and, with a hoarse caw of laughter and a flash of dark wings, the little creature, half-crow, half-man, had flitted into the branches overhead.

I sat up and reached out quickly for my sword. The smooth weight of the hilt was a comfort. Then I shook the boy awake, and Saiko, too. She opened her eyes, moaned, and shivered. "Oh. It's cold. Is it—it's morning? Do we have any food?"

I was tempted to slap her. "This isn't a picnic," I growled.

"I know." Saiko dropped her gaze modestly. "Please forgive my rudeness."

I had a lot more than rudeness to forgive her for, and I didn't plan to do it. She sat there, eyes meekly downcast, gingerly rubbing one foot. I stripped off my sandals and thrust them at her. To her credit (and I was willing to count very little to her credit, just then), she hesitated to take them.

"Put them on," I snapped. "I can walk barefoot. You can't. And the sandals won't fit him." I waved a hand at the boy, who was sitting up nearby, rubbing his face and eyeing the trees and brush around us nervously. "You." I frowned at him. "What's your name?"

"Ichiro," he said hesitantly, as if he were afraid it might be the wrong answer.

"Your *other* name," I insisted.

Now he sounded even more apologetic. "Kashihara."

I groaned. "You're a Kashihara?" But of course he was. Because that was the only thing that could make this mission any worse.

The Kashihara brothers had divided the province between them like a sweet rice cake. Their feuds and alliances had kept samurai and soldiers and ninjas, too, employed for years.

Quickly, my brain sorted through everything I'd learned about the family. There had been three brothers, until recently. One had died not many months ago. And he had been the only one of the three to produce any children.

One girl. And one boy, who would inherit all that the Kashihara family had to leave.

I was stranded in the wilderness with the sole heir of the most powerful family for a hundred miles. And I could think of only one thing to do with him.

"Well, Kashihara Ichiro," I said, drawing in a deep breath. "Now we're—"

Then Ichiro did something that startled me so much I stopped talking. He turned toward me, got on his knees, and bowed, bringing his forehead down completely to the ground.

Most samurai's sons or little lordlings would have swallowed a razor rather than kneel to a ninja. Particularly one who happened to be a girl. And this one was a Kashihara. Bending his neck for me?

"Your name is Kata?" he said, courteously, as he rose again. "My sister told me."

I glanced at Saiko, who was now slipping on my second

sandal. She was a Kashihara, too. Which I supposed was the reason I was in this predicament. Saiko must have known, or suspected, that it was her little brother who was not supposed to wake up in the morning, and she had decided to do something about it.

"You saved my life," Ichiro said. "My thanks to you."

I looked blankly at him for a heartbeat or two, while something hot and uncomfortable writhed and coiled in my gut.

It was shame.

Well, I should've felt ashamed, certainly. I'd failed in my very first mission. The living proof of that—yes, that was the point, *living*—stood before me.

The boy's face was open, and pleasant, and a little puzzled about why I was staring at him. He was truly grateful. He was grateful to *me*.

"I haven't saved anyone yet," I said shortly, and reached down a hand to pull Saiko to her feet. "No more resting. Time to go."

As we moved under the trees once more, something bounced off the top of my head and hit the ground in front of me. A pinecone.

I looked up, and the second one hit my nose.

A faint snicker drifted down from the tree above me, but nothing stirred the dusky green needles.

I broke into a jog, dodging between trunks. Saiko followed. The boy brought up the rear.

I didn't have the heart to tell him he'd just been kidnapped.

EIGHT

I kept us to back roads and hunters' trails, judging our direction by the angle of the sun and the shadows when I found myself in unfamiliar territory. It took longer, but it kept us out of sight. Mounted men might be pursuing us on the roads, but they were unlikely to track us on winding paths so narrow that we walked in single file.

Kiku was on watch when we arrived, at last, at the school. She was there to pull the gate open and let us stumble in, our shadows stretching out long before us in the late afternoon light.

"What are you doing here?" she gasped, wide-eyed as she took in the sight of us. The gate clanged shut and Saiko slid into a graceful heap on the ground.

We'd been so *slow*. I could have covered the distance in half the time, and even Ichiro could probably have moved quicker. But the best pace Saiko could manage seemed like a crawl to me. So many times I'd been tempted to leave her by the path, but the truth was, I needed her. This daughter of the Kashiharas could help explain to Madame how my assassination had turned into a kidnapping.

Girls who had been sparring all over the yard turned to stare at the three of us. Fuku aimed one last blow at Masako's head that could have knocked her senseless, but Masako parried it without a glance—frankly, a better move than I had thought her capable of. She left Fuku standing and scowling as she ran across the yard to us.

"Where's Madame?" I demanded, swaying a little on my feet. I wanted to face her now. To learn my fate this instant would be better than to wait, and wonder, and dread.

Besides, as Madame decided what to do to me, she could also decide what to do about Ichiro and Saiko. I felt like I'd been dragging my two boulders uphill for miles. At last I was going to heave the burden onto someone else's shoulders.

"She's not here," Masako answered.

"Not *here*?"

I could not believe it. All this long day, I'd been rehearsing my explanation to Madame, picturing her face, anticipating her wrath. And now she wasn't *here*?

"A samurai came at the hour of the hare. He wore the dragonfly." Masako's gaze was shifting from me to Ichiro to Saiko. "She left with him."

Of course. It shouldn't have come as a surprise that Madame had left with a warrior bearing the Kashihara dragonfly. Her client's midnight peace had been broken by explosions in his garden, and where he'd been expecting a corpse, he'd found an empty futon and an open window. Naturally he'd come seeking an explanation. Madame must have gone with him to the castle to see what she could discover.

"She took one of the instructors with her," Masako went on.

"Willow or The Boulder?" I asked.

Quick amusement flickered in Masako's eyes. "Willow. That's what I call her too. But I call him—"

The main door of the house slid open.

"Huge," Masako whispered, and all the girls fell silent as The Boulder stepped down into the yard, slid on his sandals, and walked toward us.

I could almost feel his gaze as it landed on me, the way a hot puff of wind pushes against your face. Then he looked briefly at Saiko, sitting on the ground, and Ichiro bending solicitously over her. And back again at me.

"Who's the boy?" he asked.

I stepped away from the brother and sister, keeping my eyes on The Boulder, and lowered my voice.

"He's ransom," I said.

I'd been supposed to kill Ichiro. I'd failed. Still, he might be of use to Madame another way. Someone wanted him dead. But he was a Kashihara, so surely he had allies or protectors who would be glad to have him back.

Glad *and* generous.

I hoped so, anyway. Madame would be receiving no fee for an assassination that had not happened, but a ransom might make up for that.

If I were very, very lucky.

Do not rely on luck. Rely on training and strength. Rely on skill.

My skill had failed me. I'd failed my training. Luck was all I had left.

"Then get him inside and keep him there," was all The Boulder said, before he turned his back on us and headed for the house.

Masako let out her breath. I raised my voice.

"Inside," I said to Ichiro, who looked up from his sister. "Saiko, go with him. Oh, somebody help her, then, if she's so *weak*," I spat furiously, as Saiko moaned at the thought of getting to her feet. "Or sit in the yard. I don't care. But you," I growled at Ichiro. *"In!"*

"Fuku, Tomiko, get the chamber under the stairs ready," Masako said briskly. "Okiko, take Saiko inside as well. No, Ozu, don't you know better than to ask Kata questions about a mission? Anyway, she's exhausted. Kata, do you want a meal or a bath or a bed first?"

Oh, a bath. Hot water and steam. I'd forgotten there was anything so marvelous in the world, and I was so grateful to Masako for suggesting it that I could have kissed her, or burst into tears.

I didn't, of course. Either one would have been ridiculous. But for that moment, despite everything, I did feel that I'd come home.

※ ※ ※

I scrubbed my skin clean with handfuls of rice bran, sloshed water over myself to rinse mud and sweat down the drain, and climbed into the wooden tub. We were lucky to have a hot spring near the school; steaming water dripped through bamboo pipes, and I could feel the aches of the last day and night starting to melt away.

I was up to my chin in hot water when Saiko came into the bathhouse, shutting the door behind her.

In the gloom and the steam, with just a white under-robe around her shoulders, she looked like a ghost. She slipped off her sandals before stepping up from the bare earth onto the wooden floor. Then she knelt by the tub where I was soaking, so that her face was on a level with mine.

"Please, Kata. I would like to explain."

Her voice was as perfect as the rest of her, every word as delicate as a chime from a silver bell.

"You don't need to explain to me," I answered, and in my own ears my words sounded as harsh as a crow's spring call. I hadn't half finished my soak, but I got out of the tub and snatched up a cotton cloth to rub myself dry.

"It's Madame you will have to explain to," I said coldly, twisting my hair to wring the water out of it. "You nearly got me killed. *You ruined my mission.*" And it had been my first. My *first.*

There was a stinging, hot pressure behind my eyes, and that made me angrier than ever. Was I going to *cry* now? Because of *her*?

No. I was not.

Saiko did not get up. She knelt at my feet, and her face, elegant and beautiful and hauntingly sad, looked up pleadingly at me through wisps of steam.

"When Madame comes back, you can talk to her," I said as viciously as I could. "Until then, don't speak a *word* to me."

I threw on my jacket and trousers. They were filthy and

I was clean, but I was too angry to care. Snatching up my sandals, I stalked outside, leaving the bathhouse to Saiko. I paused in the yard before heading for the main house. The Boulder had the rest of the girls drilling with wooden swords. He glanced at me and looked away.

Should I find a practice blade? But I wasn't a student any longer.

I wasn't a ninja either.

And clearly The Boulder wasn't going to tell me what to do. He didn't even turn his head to look at me a second time. He was going to leave me to Madame. Me and the boy I'd brought with me.

It felt as if I stood there for hours, though it could only have been a few heartbeats, before I stirred myself into motion again and walked into the house. No one stopped me. No one spoke to me. I made my way upstairs, took a mat from a cupboard, unrolled it, and lay down. All at once I was too tired even to undress. I kicked off my sandals and closed my eyes. Catching up on some of the rest I'd been denied the night before was all I could think of to do.

But for the first time in years, my sleep was not restful. In my dreams, I was alone, and I was running.

Slow. I was so *slow*! It was a huge effort of will to lift each of my feet. And now I had to turn and fight, but my sword was gone.

I threw kicks and punches in vain. The thing chasing me was never there to be hit. It was behind me, hissing in my ear. It was far away, howling. It vanished under my feet like a snake in tall grass.

It was nowhere. Everywhere. It was about to capture me. It already had.

I was good. I was the best. There was not a girl in the school who could put a blade to my throat in the practice yard. I had not felt the sting of the bamboo rod in two years.

But I could not fight *this*.

I wrenched myself awake, breathing hard. How long had I slept? I'd only meant to nap. Now the room was dark around me. The other girls were asleep on their mats, and the quiet sound of their breathing made waves in the dark air. The rhythm of it should have soothed me back to sleep.

It didn't. I'd slept too long. I was awake, even sharply alert. That dream had left me ready to fight, and there was no one to attack.

And I was hungry.

It was not the first time I'd been awake and hungry, of course. Hunger had lain down beside me most of my nights at the school. I'd never done anything about it. The kitchen was kept locked.

Of course, I knew how to pick a lock.

If Madame found out . . .

Madame was not home.

One of the girls would betray me.

Only if one of them heard me. I'd just slipped in and out of a warlord's mansion. Couldn't I manage a kitchen?

I felt possessed by a little of that giddy recklessness that had taken hold of me last night. As if I were floating, I drifted up. Barefoot, picking my way carefully over and around sleeping girls, I slipped into the hallway.

There was a black thread stretched across the top of the stairs, with tiny bells, lacquered black as well, attached. It was invisible in the dark, unless you knew just where to look. I ducked under it and padded softly down, skipping the sixth step, which had been built to creak.

At the foot of the stairs, I paused and listened. The Boulder would have laid his mat out here. I heard no breathing—he must be a quiet sleeper—but I glimpsed a bulky outline against the orange and black coals that glowed in the square fire pit, and I watched it for long enough to be sure he would not stir. At last I felt safe, turned left, and let my bare feet carry me three steps to the kitchen door.

My lockpicks, well greased and wrapped in soft, quilted silk to keep them from jangling, were still in my pocket. The lock was not difficult. Maybe Madame never dreamed that any of her girls would have the audacity to attempt it.

The door slid open, and I stepped down onto the cool, smooth dirt of the kitchen floor, closing the door behind me.

No cook or maid slept in the house, of course. Madame was not foolish enough to keep servants here overnight. They might be bribed or threatened into opening a door or leaving a shutter unlatched, clearing the way for a thief or an enemy.

All the better for my mission.

Slowly, silently, I eased open the iron door to the oven so that the dim coals inside would give me just enough light to find my way. On the other side of the room there was a bamboo pipe in one wall, with a dipper hanging from it. I filled the dipper with water, took a long, cool drink, and felt the last traces of my nightmare wash away as I swallowed.

Returning to the stone oven, I lifted a lid on a clay pot and smiled. Perfect. Soup, keeping warm for tomorrow. If the level in the pot was a finger's width lower in the morning, who would notice? With the water dipper, I scooped myself a salty, savory meal. It had mushrooms in it, and chewy seaweed. I slurped.

Something echoed the sound.

I whirled. Soup splashed across the dirt floor at my feet.

Darkness. Silence.

No, not silence. Something.

Something . . . moving.

It was a sound between a rasp and a slither. With two quick steps I moved sideways, away from the stove. I would be outlined against the glow of the fire in its innards, easy game for anyone.

Easy game for who? For what?

I held myself motionless. I would find out.

Movement betrays. Stillness conceals. Everyone's eye is on the fluttering bird. No one notices the stone.

Whatever was making that sound would be moving. That meant I could find it.

I tried to open my ears as far as I could. I poured my whole self into my listening.

I could hear my breath easing down my throat. I could hear the coals in the oven shift and sigh, hear their heat hissing into the cool air. I could hear the blood in my veins.

When the sound came again, my head turned easily toward it. I knew just where it was.

On the wall to my right was a wooden sink. Beneath it was a stone-lined drain that led to a wide bamboo pipe, so that wastewater could run out into the vegetable garden.

Something was coming up through that drain.

The pipe was much too small for a man or a woman. Even a child Ozu's size would be hard-pressed to squeeze through.

An animal, perhaps? A rat. A snake. A clever, curious badger, nosing its way toward the smell of rice.

But it did not sound exactly like any of those.

That slurping sound came again, a vile, eager little gulp. And then a strange, soft *clack-clack-clack.*

The skin on my back crawled, a chilly ripple that worked its way up my spine and into my scalp.

Whatever it was, it sounded hungry.

I'd put my sword back in the armory. I'd left my knives upstairs. There was nothing but a water dipper in my hand.

A sword is a tool, not a crutch. Use it; do not lean on it. Anything can be a weapon. A stick, a stone. A comb, a needle.

Or, of course, a cooking pot.

I laid the dipper down on the stovetop and seized the pot of soup with both hands. Then I waited, the length of one breath, until from the shadows across the room I heard small, sharp claws scrabbling against bamboo, and then the softer sound of those claws on the dirt floor.

Whatever it was, it had reached the kitchen. I threw the

pot hard and heard it thud as it hit the ground, the bamboo pipe, and—something else.

It would have been better if the soup had been boiling rather than lukewarm. Curtains of broth and showers of noodles flew everywhere. There was a squeak and more of that clacking.

This time it didn't sound hungry. It sounded angry.

I snatched up the dipper before I leaped, planning a dash across the kitchen to the door of the main room. On the second step, I slipped. A nest of noodles under my feet sent me sprawling in a slick of soupy mud.

I gasped breath back into my lungs, rolled—

—too late.

There came a quick scuttling sound that might have been made by dozens of legs all working at once, and it was on me. A snakelike weight, a long, writhing body, and those legs, too many, all grasping and pinching and scrabbling at me, while giant pincers clacked shut an inch from my face.

A centipede? But huge. Longer than I was tall, thick enough that my two hands could not quite close around it. A crawling, filthy thing that fed on mold and graves and death—only this one was trying to feed on me.

With one hand I grabbed its neck, or where its neck should have been—it was *all* neck, this thing, and trying to coil around me. I shoved the horrible head away from my face. It squealed, furious, ravenous. The mandibles snapped and sticky-soft feelers groped for my eyes. Angry claws raked the skin of my stomach and legs.

With my other hand, I gripped the water dipper tightly

and brought it down as hard as I could across the creature's head.

It squealed again, and writhed, and we were both flung about in the mud I'd made of the dirt floor. My shoulder and hip cracked hard against the platform where the cook sat to work.

I could have screamed, and ten highly trained girls, not to mention one instructor, one useless rich man's daughter, and one kidnapped boy who didn't know he'd been kidnapped, would have poured into the kitchen.

But it didn't occur to me to yell.

No ally will defend you. No army will come to your aid. No lord will protect you. Protect yourself. Be your own ally. Be your own army.

No one ever said, *Be your own lord*. But we all knew it was meant.

A ninja was for hire. A ninja served any lord. Therefore, a ninja served none.

Protect yourself.

The platform where the cook worked was just above me. He knelt there to chop and grate and mince and pound and slice and hum and whistle.

That meant there were knives, and cleavers, and mallets, laid out neatly in a row, just above my head. All I needed was to get my hands on one.

NINE

With my right hand still gripping the centipede's neck, I bashed the vile creature once more in the face with the ladle and then threw the tool away. With my left I grasped one of the feelers that were groping at my eyes and yanked as hard as I could.

The thing squealed and thrashed, and sharp claws tore at my neck, but the head reared back in panic, and I had the few seconds I needed.

Fumbling blindly along the edge of the platform, again with my left hand, I felt it—something cold and slim and sharp.

I came close to slicing my own fingers off, but in two more seconds I had the handle of a heavy knife in my hand, and I stabbed with all my strength.

The knife slid harmlessly off the centipede's slippery carapace, and its head plunged down toward my face again.

I wrestled the head back with both hands, fumbling

with the knife and nearly dropping it. While I struggled to get a firmer grip on the blade's handle without letting go of the creature's neck, it writhed a coil of its long body around my chest. I felt it suddenly cinch tight.

My breath burst out from between my lips. My ribs creaked.

Would it crush me first? Or would its fangs be in my neck while there was still breath in my lungs?

Don't hack blindly. That's for samurai on horseback. One thrust is enough for a ninja. Plan your attack. Know your target.

The thing's armor was too tough for anything but an axe. What did that leave? The most vulnerable parts of any creature—eyes, ears, mouth.

The centipede's mouth gaped. Grayish froth sizzled and dripped from its fangs into my face, stinging where it touched.

I found a good grip on the knife and thrust it with all the strength of my arm and shoulder straight into the demon's mouth.

Thick, white fluid from the wound splashed over my arm to the elbow. The centipede screeched and flailed, and my head hit the platform hard enough that dark stars burst across my vision. But then the creature flopped down on top of me, shuddered all along its length, and lay horribly, heavily still.

I shuddered, too, and fought free of its coils, shoving and kicking them away, then crawled up to the cook's platform, out of the mud, gripping the knife tightly. There I took stock of myself.

My clothes had protected me from the worst of the creature's claws. The scratches across my stomach and neck were the deepest, but even they would stop bleeding soon on their own. I'd have a bruise on my temple and a sore shoulder from hitting the platform. But I was still strong enough to fight, and that was what mattered.

My face was stinging where the demon's foamy saliva had dripped. I scrubbed at the sore spots with my sleeve and felt my shivering start to ease.

That had been no ordinary creature. It was something from the shadows, from the hidden places of the world. Something unnatural. Something *changed*.

A bakemono. A demon.

Of course I'd known there were demons in the world. But I'd never expected to meet one in the kitchen.

I'd never expected to meet a tengu in the forest, either.

Why? Why was all this happening now?

Never mind *why*. That was not the most urgent question.

What I really needed to know was: were there more?

I listened, but I could hear nothing except my own ragged, juddering breath. That would never do. I closed my eyes and deliberately let the tension in my shoulders ease. Three counts to breathe in. Five to breathe out. Again. Five to breathe in, seven to breathe out.

Listen.

A faint, fragile chime rang out. Tiny bells had been gently shaken. The sound rippled through the dark and empty rooms.

Something was in the house.

Something was on the stairs. Going up? Going down? Did it matter?

"What's happening?" asked a tentative, sleepy voice. "Is everything—"

I barreled past Ichiro where he stood in the doorway to the main room, very nearly knocking him sprawling, and took the stairs two at a time. I didn't skip the creaking sixth step. The more noise, the better.

"Wake up!" I bellowed.

Someone was already at the top of the stairs. I lifted my knife, but lowered it when I heard Masako's voice. "What was all the noise in the kitchen?" she asked, worried. "And I heard the bells. Kata, did you—"

I felt for the thin black thread. It had been broken. Each piece, strung with bells, hung limply from a nail.

"No, I didn't," I answered grimly. "Someone's in the house."

"Quiet, all of you!" Masako said sharply to the younger girls, who were crowding around.

We listened, twenty-six ears straining in the darkness.

"There's nothing." Fuku's voice came from the shadows on my left.

"Nothing didn't break the bell thread." Masako's hair whispered as she shook her head.

"Kata probably did."

"What's happening? Kata?" Ichiro was behind me on the stairs.

"You don't think I'd know if I broke a bell thread?" I growled at Fuku. My brain hurt from the effort of listening. With all this chatter, how could anyone hear the enemy?

"I don't think you'd admit it."

"What's *happening?*" Ichiro insisted.

"Nothing." Fuku was scornful. "Nothing is happening."

"Where's the instructor? Where's Huge?" Masako demanded. Everyone fell silent.

The bell thread had rung. I'd fought a giant centipede in the kitchen. Everyone in the house was awake.

I turned slowly to face the foot of the stairs.

Everyone was awake—except that still figure huddled by the fire.

It seemed to be up to me. All the girls, and Ichiro, too, stood and watched as I made my way slowly, reluctantly, down.

I skirted the dark lump on the mat, approached the hearth from the other side, grabbed a poker, and jabbed the flames into life.

My shoulders sagged with relief.

"He's not here." I looked up at the apprehensive faces on the stairs. "It's just his quilt. He's gone."

"Gone?" Masako started down, Ozu clinging to her hand. "He left? Why would he leave?"

"The door's still locked," Kazuko pointed out as the girls and Ichiro trooped down behind Masako, Saiko bringing up the rear. "Unless he went out through the kitchen."

"He wasn't upstairs," Aki said.

"Not upstairs," Okiko repeated, nodding.

"Is he in the classroom?" Kiku looked that way but didn't move to check.

I stepped away from the fire. Gingerly, I used the tip of the poker to lift the crumpled pile of silk from the mat underneath.

"No," I said. "He's not in the classroom." Or upstairs. Or outside. Somehow I was quite sure that The Boulder was not anywhere in this world, not anymore.

Everyone stared down at the mat, at the dark splotch as large as a man—a big man—that had been revealed when I lifted the quilt. Ichiro drew in a slow breath.

"We'll search the house." Masako's voice was firm, and it seemed to shake us all out of a daze. "We'll need light first. Kiku, Tomiko. Get lanterns lit. Stay together. No one is to go anywhere alone. Fuku, don't argue."

Miraculously, they did it. Even Fuku kept her mouth shut while Kiku and Tomiko hurried to get the lanterns off their shelf and light them at the fire. In the pale light glowing through the rice paper, faces were revealed: Fuku, nervous and restless; little Ozu, holding tight to Masako's hand; the twins Aki and Okiko, together as always, trading quick glances as if talking without words; Yuki, alert but not panicked; Kazuko, bouncing on the balls of her feet; Masako, sharp-eyed and watchful.

All of them took in the sight of me.

"Kata. What . . ." Masako whispered.

I cut her off. "When we get to the kitchen, you'll see."

Masako wanted to ask more, but she bit her questions back when I shook my head.

"Kiku, Tomiko, go with Yuki and check the rooms upstairs," she said briskly instead. "Fuku and Oichi, with me. Saiko, too. We'll look in the classroom. Kata, inspect the windows and the door here. Take Aki and Okiko. Kazuko, stay on the stairs. You'll be a messenger if we need one. Ozu, of course you stay with me."

For half a second I bristled—who was Masako to order me about, as if I were Ozu's age? But I had no fault to find with her plan, and we had no time to waste on arguing.

"What about me?" Ichiro asked meekly.

Masako looked baffled. What *should* we do with him—our tame hostage, our unwitting prisoner?

"Oh, come with me," I grumbled.

It didn't take long for us to check the house and gather back in the main room to report. The dormitories and the hallway upstairs: nothing. The wing with the classroom: nothing. The main room: nothing. The secret room under the stairs where we'd stowed Ichiro was empty. The screens on the windows were unbroken.

Then I led the way into the kitchen.

Nothing there, either. Except, of course, an upended pot of soup and the corpse of a centipede demon.

Everyone wanted an explanation, but I cut them off until the search was over. At last there was only one place left to look: Madame's own chamber.

We gathered together back in the main chamber and stood before her door. I gripped my knife tightly, feeling that I'd rather face a troop of mounted samurai, or another flesh-eating demon, than go into that room unbidden. It wasn't even locked. Of course it wasn't locked. The kitchen might need defending, but Madame's room? Our fear of her was a barrier better than any lock or bar.

It was Yuki who gently pushed the door open, looked back over her shoulder at us, and stepped inside. Fuku flicked a glance at me and followed. The rest of us crowded in.

No one was hiding in Madame's cupboards or beneath her low desk or under the cushions that lay on her floor.

The window screens were smooth and undamaged, the shutters latched. My skin prickled the whole time, but that was merely from imagining what Madame would say if she found we'd been in her room without her permission.

Yuki knelt before a chest much too small to hide a person, and before I could protest, slipped it open.

"What are you *doing*?" Masako whispered, alarmed.

Mutely, Yuki showed her what she had taken out—rolls of bandages and several small ceramic jars with tight-fitting lids.

"Well—in the other room, then," I told her. Medical supplies, the ones Madame kept in her room to treat training injuries. We might need them tonight, certainly. But I felt better when Yuki had closed the chest and we were all clustered around the hearth in the main room.

"Nothing. I *said*." Fuku was trying to sound disdainful, but her gaze kept skittering toward The Boulder's mat.

"What's in the kitchen is not *nothing*," Masako countered. "And something happened to—" Her gaze dropped to the mat as well. "To him."

Yuki had knelt beside me and was smearing a greasy paste from one of her little jars over the scratches on my stomach and neck.

"He probably just ran away," Fuku grumbled.

"And bled all over his mat?" Masako countered. "And locked the door behind himself?"

With a hand on my chin, Yuki turned my head gently to one side, squinting at my face. Then she took another little jar and rubbed its contents over my cheek. I hadn't realized how much it was stinging until it stopped.

"Kata could have locked the door, and—" Fuku stopped mid-sentence as I pushed Yuki's hand away and got to my feet.

"She didn't. And the instructor didn't just run." Saiko sounded certain. All eyes, even mine and Fuku's, turned toward her. Ichiro nodded.

"What do you mean?" Masako asked.

"What do you *know?*" My right hand, still holding the kitchen knife, twitched. "The two of you—"

The flames of every lantern blew out.

The darkness closed in. Our eyes had adjusted to the lantern light, and our night vision was gone. All I could see was the dimmed glow of the hearth.

"No one move." It was Masako's voice. On her knees by the hearth, she was using the poker to stir the coals into life. Faces sprang out of the darkness—startled, worried, alert, afraid. "There, now we can see. Hand those lanterns to me. Quickly."

The shutters rattled.

It wasn't wind. That would have stirred the trees outside as well. But the leaves were silent.

Something else was shaking the wooden shutters. Something was trying to lift the latches.

"Weapons." Masako's voice was low but clear. "Kata, Aki, Okiko. Go."

I snatched up a lantern and lit it at the hearth, charring one of the paper screens in my hurry. Then, with the twins on my heels, I dashed for the kitchen. No one wasted breath on words.

Through the kitchen, skidding in mud, leaping over the demon's corpse. Into the storeroom, piled high with bags of rice and millet, barrels of salted fish, baskets of radishes and eggplant. I seized hold of a section of wall, hooked my fingers in a knothole, and pulled. The wall slid aside.

A storeroom of a different type lay beyond.

I began tossing weapons back to Aki and Okiko. Staffs. Swords. Shuko for close fighting. No throwing knives; the house was too small. We'd be in danger of hitting each other. I kept a short wakizashi blade for myself.

Back to the main room. Masako had the rest of the lanterns lit again. No sound came from the windows. The squares of rice paper were white and blank in their frames.

Quickly, Masako dispatched her tiny army—Aki and Okiko to the top of the stairs, where they could listen for any signs of intrusion on the second floor. Kiku with Masako herself to Madame's room. Kiku let out a little whimper at the idea of intruding on that shrine once more, but there was another wide, shuttered window there, another point of attack.

Tomiko and Kazuko to the classroom. Fuku and Oichi to the kitchen, to watch the outside door. "And the drain!" I called out after them.

Yuki and me in the main room. "And Saiko," Masako ordered.

I shook my head. "Take her with you."

"You might need—"

"I don't want her at my back!"

Masako nodded after one glance at my face. "Saiko,

90

with me. What's your name—Ichiro? You look after Ozu."

"I can fight!" Ichiro looked indignant. When girls his own age were drawing swords and strapping clawed shuko over their knuckles, being a nursemaid was a lot for the Kashihara heir to swallow.

"You may have to." Masako threw him a sword, which he caught deftly enough in a hand that I noticed had been neatly bandaged. "But for now I don't know how to use you. Ozu, be brave, pet—you know how. Scatter, girls!"

At every point of entry, we waited.

Nothing happened.

I shifted my grip on my sword's hilt, rolled my shoulders to keep them loose, and waited.

Nothing happened.

Eyes on the window. Breathing soundlessly. Ears not strained, but alert.

Without looking, I could feel Yuki beside me. She was best at herbs and medicines and potions, but she could still handle the staff she'd chosen as a weapon. If I had my choice, I'd pick her to slip poison into a cup rather than to have at my back in a melee, but she would do.

Ichiro had pulled Ozu over by the staircase, out of the line of sight from the window. The shutter outside creaked.

Of course Madame would make sure that all her shutters creaked. Anyone coming into this house would not do so in silence.

Something poked through the screen.

It was thin and black and it didn't poke far. Just enough to pull downward, slitting the rice paper as it went.

I held up a hand to Yuki, pointed at myself. She nodded.

The sharp black thing reached through the slit it had made. It was—I did not know what it was. A long, gnarled, knobbed, clawed finger? It grew and stretched like a root. It flexed like a snake.

I stepped silently nearer, raised my sword, and sliced it off.

The blood that spurted out was smoking hot, and the scream from outside roiled my guts and nearly made my eardrums bleed. And then five—ten—a dozen of those fingers punctured the screen, and Yuki was beside me, swinging her staff overhead and slamming it down as I sliced and stabbed.

Fuku shouted from the kitchen. "The door! Brace it!"

The paper of the screen before me was in shreds, but still I could not see much of what was outside. The firelight glinted off a handful of smooth scales. I hacked off a clump of matted, stinking fur.

Ozu shrieked.

I whirled to see something swooping down from the second floor on wide wings knitted out of cobwebs and midnight. At the bottom of the stairs, Ozu and Ichiro ducked as the thing stretched out sleek black talons, talons that might have snagged a bell thread not so long ago.

Hot breath as foul as the grave rolled over me, making me gag, and wrenching my attention back to my own fight. I stabbed straight into a black mouth, my blade sliding between white fangs that nearly took my hand off at the wrist. Out of the corner of my eye I saw Ichiro's sword sweep up over his head, but before he could touch his enemy, Ozu snatched up a lantern that had been left by the hearth and flung it with all the strength in her wiry little body straight at the creature plunging down on the two of them.

Light flared. The bakemono writhed and rippled in the air like smoke caught in a strong breeze. I wrenched my blade free, and Yuki jabbed with her staff, smashing through the remnants of the window frame to score a direct hit on what was left of our opponent's face—if that was a face, if the thing *had* a face.

Something from Madame's room keened like a hunting hawk. "There!" Masako called out. "Watch it, *there!*"

I stabbed again, hard, right where Yuki had struck, but my sword sliced through nothing and I nearly lost my balance, braced to meet resistance that didn't come. How could I fight something that no longer seemed to be there?

I snatched up a lantern and thrust it between two splintered wooden slats and out into the night. I could see nothing. The thing had melted away, as if the darkness had taken it, piece by piece.

Yuki seized my shoulder, pulled me back, and scowled at me. She slapped at my arm, as if she were asking, "Don't you want to keep that?"

I shrugged. "It's gone."

"Ours, too. Yuki, we need you." Masako was at the door to Madame's room. Kiku was leaning against her. The younger girl's arm was bloody from shoulder to fingertips.

Ichiro was stamping on the wreckage of the paper lantern. There was no sign at all of the flying creature that had come down the stairs. Ozu ran to throw herself on Masako as the older girl eased Kiku down by the hearth.

"It was a bird!" Kiku chattered, shivering. "I *think* it was a bird! It was huge! Its beak came right through the screen! Will it be back? Do you think it will be back? Masako, what if it comes back?"

"Let's not give it the chance," I said, and knelt. One of the tatami mats that lay across the floor was askew, its corner overlapping its neighbor. I peeled that corner back. Under it was a trapdoor.

It probably wasn't the only one in the house. But it was the only one all of the girls knew about. It connected to an underground tunnel that led to a hole beneath the hedge. Perfect for escape. Or ambush.

"No," Masako said.

From where I knelt, I looked up at her. My sword was still in my hand.

"To strike blindly is to lose," she said. "We don't know what we're fighting."

"We can still *fight*." I laid a hand on the trapdoor's latch. "Better than waiting here like frightened birds in a nest."

All the girls were watching. Fuku, standing in the doorway to the kitchen, had a smirking smile on her face.

The latch to the trapdoor moved easily under my

fingertips. It was open. Had I turned it without noticing, my eyes on Masako?

"Kata," Masako insisted. "*No.*"

I was sure I hadn't.

"*You* shouldn't"—Ichiro's voice startled everyone. Saiko shook her head. But the boy didn't stop talking, and he didn't take his eyes from me—"go. If anyone does. You're the one they're after."

"Explain." I was back on my feet, and my sword felt light in my hand, like a bird longing to fly. "They're after *me? Why?*"

The trapdoor at my feet exploded.

Heavy planks of wood burst into splinters and sawdust. Girls were screaming. The blast flung me to the floor, and I was rolling. I caught a glimpse of Masako's face, half of it red with blood from forehead to chin. I saw Ichiro snatch Ozu and turn, falling to his knees, his back between her and danger.

Something grabbed my right ankle.

It was a fierce grip, and cold as a fetter of steel, dragging me backward, facedown along the floor. I groped for a handhold, but my fingers found nothing but slippery, flimsy mats. My sword—where was it? There, on the floor—beyond my grasp.

What *had* me?

I writhed and twisted, craned my neck, and saw.

My mind could not assemble what my eyes were seeing into a single creature. Impossibly long arms. Impossibly huge mouth. Tattered flesh, all gray and white, that seemed to be unraveling like poorly woven cloth. If it had eyes, I could not see them. If it had a heart, I did not know where.

If hunger had a body, it would look like this. And The Boulder hadn't been enough of a meal for it. It wanted me.

Someone had an arm around my chest and was trying to pull me backward. My foot was going to snap off at the ankle. I kicked with my free leg, but it was no use. The girl holding me was being pulled right along the floor with me.

Masako's sword lifted, a red-gold slash in the dark air, and came down. Once. Twice.

The thing howled and let go. I tried to roll free, but I was in a tangle with my would-be rescuer, and by the time I'd shoved myself away, snatched up my sword, and spun on my knees to face whatever was attacking me, the thing was—

—melting?

Ropes and rags of gray-white flesh were dissolving into shreds of clammy fog that crawled blindly about on the floor as if searching for help. Masako stood with her sword raised, and I braced myself, but we had nothing left to fight. The last of the mist vanished with a stench like rotting leaves, cold damp earth, age and decay.

"Find something—" Masako waved at the shattered trapdoor and then clapped a hand to her bloody forehead. "Cover that hole." She sat down abruptly on the floor. Yuki was at her side in an instant.

"That chest over there," said the girl sitting on the floor behind me, the one who'd tried to drag me away from the demon's grasp.

I recognized the voice.

Saiko.

I threw myself on her and locked my hands around her throat.

TEN

The other girls pulled me off of Saiko quickly, and I wasn't actually trying to hurt her. If I'd been trying, I would have succeeded. But being attacked by a demon for the second time in one night had soured my temper, and lovely little Saiko had much to answer for.

I'd lived fifteen years without demons trying to eat me. It was only after I'd met this girl and her brother that I had become a target.

I shrugged Oichi's hand off my shoulder and pulled my arm out of Aki's grasp. "All right, I won't," I growled, and I wheeled to face Ichiro instead of his pretty, deceitful sister. "You said the demons were after me. *Why?*"

"In your pocket," Ichiro said simply. "Look."

I did not know what to think of him. He stood there, in his loose jacket and trousers, somehow managing to look as ordinary as a peasant boy and as dignified as a prince. He looked trustworthy. But then, Saiko looked meek and innocent. I knew better than to believe a face was anything more than a mask.

As Aki and Okiko maneuvered a heavy chest over the gaping hole in the floor where the trapdoor had been, I slipped a hand cautiously inside my jacket. I felt something smooth and hard and round, like a pebble from the sea floor, and I drew it out.

A pearl, encircled by a band of gold, the whole thing a bit smaller than the circle made by my thumb and forefinger. There was a hole in the golden ring, trailing a short length of the thin chain that had snapped when Ichiro yanked it off his neck. It lay in my palm more heavily than it should, as if something beyond its own density weighed it down. Centuries of age, perhaps. Or maybe . . .

Something dry and brown was smeared across the milky whiteness of the pearl. Blood.

"I thought I was going to fall," Ichiro explained. "So I gave it to you."

My eyes were on Ichiro. Everyone's were. But I could not miss the way Saiko was looking at her brother. Her glare could have set him on fire.

I remembered how Ichiro had dangled from my hands for a moment at the top of the castle wall. He'd cared more about this jewel than he had about his life.

"And my hand was bleeding," he finished. "So . . ."

He shrugged. He seemed to think that everything made sense now.

I looked to Saiko, who still knelt on the floor, rubbing her throat. She closed her eyes and sighed, perhaps letting some frustration go.

"My mother told me once that a god gave it to our family," she said, as if she were used to filling in Ichiro's gaps. "So long ago no one can remember. She said that it was a gift, and a burden. That it can do things. And that it—calls to things."

"Things?" I pressed.

She waved a graceful hand at the chaos around us—splintered floor, broken window frames, tattered paper screens. "It passed to Ichiro a few months ago, when our father was killed."

"Killed how?" I wanted details. I needed to understand.

"Bandits attacked him on the road," Ichiro answered, his voice flat. "Our uncle brought the pearl to me. There was—" He faltered. "Blood was on it. Uncle Hikosane said our father held it and willed it to me with his last breath."

"Blood." I understood now. "Blood allows it to—"

"To pass to a new owner." Saiko nodded. "That is how it has always been done in our family. From father to son." Something flickered through her dark eyes and was gone in an instant. "When a father thinks his oldest son is ready, he'll draw his own blood and hand the pearl to him. But, of course, there is another way. As our uncle knew."

"Sister, what are you saying?" Slow shock was dawning on Ichiro's face.

"If an owner dies with the pearl in his possession, then it is free to be taken." Saiko didn't take her eyes from her brother. "Taken by anyone *except* the killer. Our uncle wanted Ichiro dead, so that the pearl could pass to him."

Ichiro was shaking his head. "No. No, it can't be Uncle Hikosane, sister. He took me in—he took us both in. He's been good to us."

"To you."

"Saiko. Please."

"You trust much too easily, little brother. He was kind to you? Of course he was. You're the boy, the heir." Disdain twisted Saiko's mouth. "But he barely noticed my existence, and that gave me the chance to watch him. And I've never seen a colder heart." Her gaze moved briefly around the room. "Not even here."

"But he, he brought the pearl to me!" Ichiro was stumbling over his words, as if arguing was not one of his skills. "You know he did. He took it from—" The boy swallowed. "Father was dead. Uncle Hikosane could have kept the pearl for himself, but he brought it straight to me."

"Ichiro, it was Daigoro who brought me here." Saiko was impatient. "He told me it was on Hikosane's orders, and that our uncle wanted me to do whatever I was told. You know what I was told."

"That doesn't mean it was true," Ichiro said a little wildly. "Daigoro could have been lying. How do you know he didn't want the pearl himself?"

"You think Daigoro disobeyed our uncle? He's been Hikosane's faithful retainer for years. He's like a dog; he follows any command."

"But you don't," I interrupted. I didn't care as much as these two exactly who it was that wanted the boy dead; I had other things on my mind. "You knew your brother was the target all along," I said to Saiko. "And so you decided to save him." To save him by ruining my first mission. No, I had not forgotten that.

She shook her head. "Not until I saw Ichiro sleeping there. I only knew my uncle wanted someone—removed. I wondered who. I admit that. But I did not know."

"And now the pearl is yours," Ichiro said, turning to me. "I'm sorry."

He glanced sideways. I was not sure whether his apology was meant for Saiko or me.

"It calls to things. As my sister said," he went on. "Ghosts and demons. Bakemono. Creatures. Monsters. They're drawn to it. As if they're . . ." He paused. "*Hungry* for it."

"The way a moth hungers for light," Saiko said, with her eyes on me. "As long as you have it, they'll come after you."

*　*　*

I kept a cautious eye on the road, the yard, and the fields out back the next morning, but no tengu seemed to be lurking in the trees, no giant centipedes slithering up from the well, and no nameless, faceless creatures of hunger hiding behind the stables.

All I could see was sunrise, the time for three young travelers to set off on a journey.

Last night I had sat by the hearth, holding the pearl in both hands as the girls and Ichiro talked and argued and wondered. Their tangled, crisscrossed words seemed to weave a net in the dark air over and around me, until I felt as if I were under the sea myself, where the pearl had once been. Floating. Drifting. Loose and unanchored, with firm ground nowhere in sight.

"Destroy it," Masako said. "Cast it into the fire."

"No!" Saiko sounded alarmed. "We don't—we don't know what might happen if we did that. What we might set free."

"Do pearls even burn?" someone else asked.

"Throw it into the ocean, then," Masako countered.

"It could wash up on shore. Or get caught in a fisherman's net." Ichiro didn't like that idea. "You can't just throw it away. Another demon might get hold of it. Or if Kata were to die, then the next person to pick it up—"

"But she can't stay here with it!" Fuku's sharp whine was irritating to my ear. "Are we supposed to fight off monsters every night?"

"Bakemono are stirring now because of the blood," Ichiro explained. "Because the pearl has a new owner. It's—awake now, I suppose. In a way. As long as Kata keeps the pearl safe, they'll settle back down after a while. Mostly."

"Mostly?" Kiku sounded alarmed.

"In a while? How long is a while?" Fuku demanded.

"I don't know." Ichiro sounded unhappy. "There are ceremonies and things you can do to keep the demons away, but . . ."

"But *what*?" Fuku demanded.

"But I don't know how to do them."

"Well, who *does* know?" she persisted.

There was a pause.

"Uncle Hikosane might . . ." Ichiro started to say.

"Ichiro, he plotted to kill you," Saiko snapped.

"We don't *know* that."

"I know it well enough. Fine, then. Even if it *is* Daigoro and not our uncle who wants you dead, we can't go back to that castle."

"Uncle Yoshisane, then," Ichiro said.

Saiko sighed, perhaps reluctant, and nodded.

"Who?" Masako asked.

"Uncle Yoshisane," Ichiro repeated. "Our father's other brother. I think he might help us. He doesn't like Uncle Hikosane. Much."

"Might?" Masako questioned.

"In any case, we can't—" Ichiro looked up, as if he'd taken new courage. "We can't just stay here."

"But the demons will follow Kata wherever she goes," Masako objected. "As long as she has this thing!"

"Most of them can't. They're tied to their places. A river sprit must stay near its river. Even tengu have their own territory. If we keep moving, we'll be safer."

"You're sure?" Masako pressed.

Ichiro shrugged. He looked very young. "I think so."

"There's one other way." Saiko's voice seemed to startle us all. I glanced up, briefly. She was looking right at me.

At my hands, and at what was cupped between them.

"You could give it away."

My hands tightened into fists.

"It's a burden to you. A danger. You do not need to bear it. It was given to our family. A samurai family. Not

104

someone like—" She paused and decided not to finish her thought as the face of every girl around the fire hardened slightly. "I mean to say, you can let it go, with honor. Someone else can face the danger."

And of course, I could. Slice my own hand and give this thing away, as easily as Ichiro had given it to me.

Give it to whom? To one of the other girls at the school? To Madame, when she returned? To Ichiro, who was no more than a boy?

To Saiko?

She was kneeling, very upright, very still. Awaiting my reply. They all were. The nets were floating above my head.

I stowed the pearl quickly away in an inside pocket of my jacket.

Ichiro was speaking again. "Blood on it twice, sister? In just a few days' time? That can't be wise. It might awaken— well, something worse."

And Saiko bowed her head humbly, acknowledging that he was right.

But the truth was, I'd decided to keep the pearl before Ichiro had opened his mouth. And Saiko, who had been watching me so closely, knew that perfectly well.

A gift from a god? It might be dangerous, but it might be valuable as well. There was no reason to simply give it away before I learned the truth about how much it was worth.

And I could face danger. I'd been trained to do that all my life.

"Your uncle—your *other* uncle—is Kashihara Yoshisane?"

I said to Ichiro, keeping my eyes away from his sister.

A nod. "He lives in—"

"The next province," I interrupted. "We'll need to cross the river and make it through the mountain pass. Three days' travel." I stood. "We'll leave at dawn."

※ ※ ※

Perhaps we should have left in the middle of the night, even with the darkness outside full of demons. How much worse could demons be than Madame?

The second Madame walked through the school gates, every chance of escape would be lost. Every chance of my keeping the pearl as well. I had to hope she'd stayed the night at the castle of Ichiro's uncle and would not return until the morning was well advanced.

The moment gray light began to glow outside the ruined shutters, I was rousting Saiko and Ichiro from their beds. Stars were still glimmering faintly in the west as I waited in the yard for them to join me.

It had not been two full days since I'd left the school on my first mission, a student no longer, a ninja at last.

And now? I had another mission, I supposed. I had a castle town to reach and enemies to face. With that in mind, I quickly scanned the dirt of the practice yard, looking for any tracks from what had attacked us last night. It would be useful to get some clues about what, exactly, we might be fighting.

But a hard rain just before dawn had washed most of the traces away. All that was left were some vague furrows in the mud beneath the windows that told me something large and heavy had stood there. And some perfectly ordinary prints where a small stray dog must have sniffed around the door after the rain was finished.

It seemed almost right that no readable prints would be left to be seen in the clear light of day. Last night had not been ordinary life, had nothing to do with the pale sun in the sky, the wisps of fog rising from the rice paddies, the flies buzzing around the stable. Last night had been something out of a legend. One that did not belong to me.

Fighting demons was a job for an emperor's son. Or at least a samurai or a warrior monk. No ninja was ever the hero of a story like that.

"Rice," an urgent voice behind me said, and when I turned Masako thrust a bundle wrapped in a large cotton cloth into my hands. "A pot. A little miso and some other things for soup."

I took the pack from her. It was enough to keep us going for a day or two, and I had a few copper coins in my pockets as well, given to me for my mission in case the first plan went awry and I needed to bribe a servant or buy some information. Back when I'd *had* a mission. Back when my life had been hard, but more or less what I'd expected.

"Yuki put in some bandages, too, and some of that salve."

I nodded.

"You don't—" Masako sounded worried. "Kata, you don't have to leave. We'd find a way to defend ourselves. We did it last night. And when Madame comes back . . ."

When Madame came back and learned about the pearl, she would do anything to get it for her own—including slicing my hand off at the wrist.

I shook my head. "We have to go. How's Kiku's arm?"

"She hurts. But Yuki's not worried. It will heal. She's given her some plum wine."

I nodded again.

"Madame." Masako leaned closer and lowered her voice. "Kata. What will we tell Madame?"

"The truth."

Masako looked more worried still. "But she'll—"

"She'll come after us anyway," I told her. "She'll guess where we're going, or she'll find our trail. If you try to deceive her, it won't help me, and all of you will suffer. Just tell her. Or let Fuku do it. I'll have a few hours' start."

"Will that be enough?"

"I'll make it enough," I answered grimly.

But that wasn't all. There were more words I needed to say. It was strangely hard to force them out of my throat.

"Last night—" I croaked.

There, two words. Masako lifted her eyebrows helpfully and waited for more.

"You were—" Curses. Two more words and I was stuck again.

Didn't I have an ounce of courage? Could I face soldiers and demons, could I infiltrate an enemy's castle, but not admit my own blunders?

"You were our general," I said at last. "They fought for you." I swallowed the bitter taste of my own misjudgments, years of them. "They would not have fought like that for me."

To my surprise, Masako reached out and took me in her arms, as a sister might.

I'd had a sister, long ago. For a moment I held Masako tightly.

"I won't ask you to come back," she said, low in my ear. "Don't. If you get away, stay. But send us word, Kata, if you can. And keep safe."

ELEVEN

Our few hours' start was slipping rapidly away as we walked past farmers at work in their fields, past villages too small to have names. Ichiro could keep up with me as long as I didn't run, but every time I glanced back over my shoulder, Saiko was farther behind.

I sighed and slackened my pace a little more. "So. If we keep moving, the demons won't attack?" I asked the boy.

He nodded, a little breathless.

"What about the night? How long can we rest?"

"I don't know," he puffed.

I slowed down yet more. "Well, when you inherited this thing, how did you keep from being eaten by demons? There were ceremonies? Isn't that what you said?"

"Yes. I mean, I don't know."

I turned to him with growing anger. Was he being unhelpful on purpose?

He shook his head. "My uncle brought the pearl to

me. Hikosane, I mean. It was at night. He just—"The boy swallowed. "Handed it to me. And told me. That my father. Was dead."

Well, so was mine. With wars and feuds and skirmishes boiling over in every province, with bandits in the mountains and little enough law left in villages and towns, a dead father was nothing out of the ordinary.

"And then?" I prompted impatiently.

"He took me to a temple. For about three days, I think. There were a lot of prayers and some rituals. I didn't have to do anything but sit. I didn't pay much attention."

His head was down; I could not see his face. And we did not have a temple handy, nor three days to spare. As slowly as Saiko was walking, we did not have two *minutes* to spare. I would have to do something about that. But for the moment I sighed again and sat down on a roadside stone, listening to the frogs croak from the ponds in the rice fields and waiting for Saiko to catch up.

"What about your mother?" I asked Ichiro.

He blinked at me. "What?"

"You said your father died. What about your mother?"

"She died when I was born." His eyes went to Saiko, still toiling her way along the road. "My sister remembers her a little. I don't." He looked out at the women in the fields, ankle-deep in mud, making their way with their hoes from row to row. It was what women everywhere did. It was what my own mother had done.

A child wearing nothing but mud toddled up to one of the women. She fended the brat off with one hand but then

111

gave in and snatched it up for a hug, mud and all.

Strange, the way that sight, or maybe Ichiro's sigh, so quiet he probably thought I had not heard, shook a memory loose deep inside me. Cold mud nearly up to my knees, and the sharp green of young rice plants close to my eyes. And over all, the blue vault of the sky, glowing as it does only in the spring, scrubbed clean with the rain and polished by the sun.

Against that blue, a face smiling so widely that the narrow cheeks looked plump and dimpled, just at the sight of me.

I did my best to slam a door shut on the face inside my mind. It was not safe to think of it. I had learned that these moments of memory were invariably followed by others.

Hiding beneath those same vivid green leaves, feeling the ground underneath me shaking. It was the hoofbeats from galloping horses that made it tremble, as if the earth were as afraid as I was.

Smoke. Screaming.

Walking barefoot on roads that never ended. Stealing moldy radishes and soggy greens out of a trash heap. Sleeping curled up in a hard knot by the roadside with a crust of burnt rice in my fist, saving it until morning.

That was where Madame had found me. And why had I let this come back to trouble me now? Why should brown mud, blue sky, green leaves sting me with such a sense of loss? What had been taken from me? Nothing I could truly remember. Nothing I'd ever grieved for. Madame had told me once I'd been the only girl she'd taken in who'd never cried.

"So you both went to live in your uncle's household, after your father died?" I asked Ichiro, my voice a bit more patient.

He nodded without looking at me. "My other uncle, Yoshisane—he wanted us to come and live with him. I heard the two of them arguing. But Uncle Hikosane is the oldest brother, now that my father is dead. He said it was his right to raise me. I'm the only boy, you know. The heir."

Lord Hikosane's house could not have been much of a refuge for either of them, I thought. Madame Chiyome's had probably been a kinder shelter.

Ichiro was frowning. "I think—I think Saiko must be wrong," he said thoughtfully. "About Uncle Hikosane. He never paid her much mind. She's a girl. But he *did* take her in, and me as well. And he brought the pearl to me. He can't be—like that. Not as bad as she thinks."

"Do you want to go back to him, then?" I asked bluntly. "It wouldn't be hard. You can sit here on this stone, and his men will probably find you within the day. I won't stop you."

Ichiro was quiet for a little while. Then he shook his head.

His sister caught up with us at last, and we went on.

Our road was in no hurry, even if we were; it wound us past endless fields of rice and millet and through villages too small to have names. And everywhere we went, past women working in the rice paddies or old men walking behind ox carts or children splashing in ditches, people's heads lifted and their eyes widened.

We had found Saiko a broad-brimmed straw hat to wear against the sun's glare, but she'd taken it off for the twentieth time to smooth her hair back behind her ears.

"Keep your hat on!" I ordered under my breath. "Don't you see people looking at you?"

She pulled the hat down over her eyes. "I can't help my face," she protested.

I was tempted to smear a handful of mud across it. "No, but you could help your—your—"

How she kept her steps small, her feet close together? How she lifted the hem of her robe as she stepped across a puddle, as if she wore seven layers of silk and not one of rough cotton? No, she probably couldn't help those things.

She had on a dark blue kimono from the school's stores, shabby and plain. Straw sandals on her bare feet. Her hair under her hat was slipping loose from its braid. And she looked . . . Well, like an empress's daughter in disguise. And a poor disguise at that.

Ichiro was not much better. Perhaps he wouldn't catch a stranger's eye, the way Saiko did. But if anyone stopped to look at him, they would not be able to help seeing how boldly he walked. How he kept his chin up and his gaze forward. How he didn't hunch his shoulders or bow his head when we met someone on the road, just in case the passerby was of higher rank and would give him a kick if he didn't.

I could stride like a nobleman as well, if I needed to. I could also limp like a beggar or drift like a nun with her mind on her meditation. A ninja learned to slide as easily from caste to caste as a fish darting from warm to cool water.

But these two had never learned. They could not look like anyone but themselves. Which meant that neither of them could look the slightest bit like a peasant, no matter what they wore.

Strangers were rare enough in these little villages. Two strangers who looked like these siblings—they'd be remembered.

Perhaps that was something I could use.

About midway through the hour of the horse, when the sun was getting high, we stopped at a farmhouse to buy some rice and pickles, saving our supplies for later. A kindly farmer's wife smiled at us, patted Saiko's cheek, and gave us three small cakes she'd just made because "it was a pleasure to see such a pretty girl."

I snorted very softly.

"Never mind, sweet, your father will find you a good husband, too!" she consoled me before she took a closer look at my face. Then she sighed, offered me an unconvincing smile that showed off her three remaining teeth, and slipped a little more rice into my bowl.

I swallowed it in one gulp and got to my feet. Saiko delicately patted her lips clean with her fingers as I counted out a few copper coins for our meal. "How much farther to the ford, Kata?" she asked. Then she gasped, because my foot had connected sharply with her ankle.

I herded her and her brother out the door. "If you can't be intelligent, can you at least be quiet?" I snarled, not quite under my breath.

"You didn't have to kick so hard," Saiko protested once

we were back on the road, drawing up one leg to rub her ankle.

"It needed to look convincing," I said, trying to hide the fact that it had been just a little satisfying as well.

"But why did you want her to say that about the ford?" Ichiro asked, as his sister limped after us.

"Yes, why bother to say it?" Saiko added. "It's the only way across the river, after all."

"If you can keep up, you'll find out."

Our road took us back and forth across a steep slope, and neither of them questioned me further; they needed their breath for climbing. Now more than ever, we could not afford to be too slow.

We'd reached the shade of a small stand of trees when I looked back and saw what I had feared—a dust cloud moving fast along the road behind us.

Inside that dust cloud, I could spot horse's heads—three of them. And three helmets. Armed samurai, Kashihara retainers, no doubt. Sent by Lord Hikosane and searching for us.

Fear, at last, gave Saiko's feet speed. But I didn't let her run, or Ichiro, either. Right now, we were only three peasant children walking along the road. Running would turn us into targets.

It took the men perhaps fifteen minutes to reach the hut where we'd stopped for food. By that time we'd rounded the next switchback and were working our way along a new stretch of slope, still in full view of the riders below. With quick glances, I could see two of them dismount and vanish inside the hut. One stayed with the horses.

The village wife who'd fed us would tell them that the pretty girl and her two companions were headed for the ford. I found myself hoping she'd tell them quickly, before they broke any of her few possessions. Or her bones.

Walk. Keep walking. Don't stop. Don't run.

How many hours had I spent poring over maps of this district, drawing them from memory, earning a slap for the slightest mistake? It was useful now. We had reached a hunting trail that branched off from the main road, heading straight up the hillside. I sent Saiko and Ichiro before me, a hands-and-knees scramble.

The samurai below were remounting. I wrenched a leafy branch off a tree and used it to brush out our tracks on the dirt of the roadside. Then—I murmured fervent thanks to the spirit of the mountain—I saw what I needed. A cedar sapling had fallen, the rocky ground too shallow for its roots. I grabbed it and heaved the entire thing over the path behind me, just where it met the road.

Men on horseback, riding quickly, men who did not know this road well, might miss the trail. Might ride right past it.

Please.

Ichiro and Saiko were crawling into the underbrush. Good. I yanked my short sword from my pack, heaved myself up a little rocky outcrop that overlooked the road, and dropped flat in the dry grass.

Carefully, I edged forward, so that I could see the road,

perhaps six or seven feet below. But I could not be seen.

The horsemen were coming. I could hear the thump of hooves on packed dirt.

I had two throwing knives, one up each sleeve. My left hand was not quite as strong as my right, but I'd have to do my best. Slowly, slowly, I drew my sword. The oiled metal slid noiselessly from its sheath. I laid it on the dusty grass beside me and gripped a knife in each hand.

I could hear more than hoofbeats now—the heavy breathing and snorting of horses working hard, the creak and clatter of armor and saddlery. They'd eased from a canter into a walk as the slope steepened.

Horses could not make it up the narrow hunting trail. If these samurai spotted it, they'd have to dismount. And I'd have to be quick.

A knife for the first, and the same for the second. If the third had any sense, he'd leave his comrades and race back to his horse, in order to get word of us to his master. I'd have to stop him before he did that. I'd have to hope that, like most samurai, he cared more for honor than sense, and that he would stay to fight.

But it would be so much better if they never saw the trail at all.

I'd been trained to fight all my life. But even more, I'd been trained *not* to fight.

Run. Hide. Escape. Only fight if you must. And only fight if you can win.

This time I wasn't sure that I could win.

They were close now. I could see the lacquer of their

armor, the deep colors beneath the road dust—blue, red, brown. I could see the black lacing that tied the plates of armor together, and the dragonfly emblem each man wore on his shoulder. They had bows strapped to their saddles, quivers on their backs. One had taken off his helmet in the heat. I saw his right ear—or what was left of it.

Then—unbelievably, maddeningly—I heard Saiko sneeze.

If I'd heard it, could the samurai have missed it? It was such a human noise. Nothing an animal would make.

If they'd heard, they'd stop. They'd search. They'd find the trail.

Two knives, one sword, and one chance. One girl against three men.

How I wished the sound of that unlucky sneeze would never reach their ears.

A strange feeling washed through me—was it nerves? Was it fear? An icy shiver shook me from my scalp to my toes, and then the feeling was gone, and I was watching the backs of the three samurai as they rode on their way.

I lay motionless while the dust of their passage settled over me, coating me in fine gray grit. Then I slithered back through the grass and down to the trail.

"I couldn't help it," Saiko said humbly after she'd crawled out of her bush. "I'm sorry, Kata."

I didn't answer. What was the point? She was no ninja, never would be. She would slow me down, hinder me, and put all of us in danger until the moment I could unload her into her uncle's care. It was useless to expect anything else.

"Who was your uncle's man? The one who brought

you to the school?" I asked, instead of slapping her senseless. "The one missing half his ear?"

"Daigoro. Why?"

I jerked my chin at the road. "He's one of the ones who almost heard you sneeze."

"You see, sister!" Ichiro had crawled out of his bush, too. "It *is* Daigoro! He's trying to catch us before Uncle Hikosane does! I *told* you!" He looked absurdly happy to be the target of a samurai instead of a warlord.

"Or Hikosane sent him to find us," Saiko countered.

"We'll stay off the road," I ordered curtly, before the two of them could start arguing again. What did it matter who was chasing us? Our goal was the same—not to get caught.

"But how are we going to reach the ford?" Saiko asked.

"We're not." I looked at their baffled faces and sighed. I wasn't used to taking the time to explain myself or my choices. And yet I supposed things would be easier if these two had some idea of where we were headed. At least it would spare me from some of the questions.

"You think there's only one way across the river," I told Saiko and her brother. "Daigoro thinks so, too. You're both wrong. Those samurai will ride on to the ford, and by the time they find out we didn't go that way, it'll be too late."

Our path was clear enough to follow, but rough and rocky, and the best pace Saiko could manage seemed like a turtle's crawl to me. A lifetime of learning to bow perfectly and sip sake delicately and walk gracefully in five layers of kimono doesn't teach you much about scrambling over rocks and up slopes—or worse, down them. By the time night fell, we had only made it as far as the river.

I chose a place along the stony bank, a fair distance from the trees all around us. I wanted as much open space as I could get, so that I'd be able to see anything coming. If only I knew what we might be looking for . . .

Ordinarily I would sleep cold on a mission; building a fire in the wilderness is as obvious as shouting "Here I am!" at the top of your lungs. But it was unlikely we'd be seen by other travelers this far from the road, and I felt sure there were things out here in the darkness that did not love light. Since we'd be in one place for several hours, those things might well be stirring, according to Ichiro. So we built a small blaze and gathered enough dry wood to keep it going until dawn.

I took the first watch. Ichiro and Saiko were asleep in minutes, their nerves no match for their exhaustion.

Awake, I sat with my back to the fire, my eyes on the line of trees. I wanted to keep my night vision sharp, and looking away from the light would help.

The deep rush of the river masked most of the other sounds, but if I concentrated, I could still hear the little winged and furry and scaly creatures whose calls and scuttlings and scurryings made up the murmur of the forest. If these sounds vanished, it would be time to hide—or fight. But for now, the forest was at peace.

Idly, I let my fingers play with the stones on the bank beside me. Most were flat and gray, but scattered in among them were a few quartz pebbles, round and white as pearls.

I picked one up and rolled it between my fingers.

Round and white as pearls . . .

I had barely had time to think about it, this thing that was tucked safely in a pocket hidden inside the lining of my jacket. This thing that was making soldiers search for me and demons hunt me down.

It was dangerous, this tiny jewel, this milky white heart of the sea. Was I being a fool to keep it with me? I could have sliced my own skin and given it to Madame when she'd returned to the school. Surely she would not have punished me for failing in my mission, if I'd handed her a gift from a god.

I could have used the pearl to bargain for forgiveness. Instead I'd chosen to run. Why?

Because it could buy me something greater than forgiveness. I understood exactly why I'd kept it as I sat there, listening to the water rush past, trapped in its stony bed. This pearl could buy me freedom.

I'd never been free in my life. When I was born, I'd belonged to whatever warlord had owned my parents. After that, I'd belonged to Madame and to the instructors, a tool forged by their hands. When I got old enough, or good enough, I had always known that Madame would sell me. Then I would belong to my new owner, and my usefulness would determine my value.

I'd never dreamed of anything else. But perhaps this pearl could buy me something I had never imagined.

All I had to do was learn what it was worth, and to whom. Then I'd give it up, for a price. The right price. Gold could buy me food, and clothes, and weapons. Gold could buy me a horse or passage on a ship. Gold could buy me a home in the capital, where my skills could be for sale to anyone who had more gold to pay me.

Once I had delivered Saiko and Ichiro safely to their uncle's care, I could disappear, and take the pearl with me. My life could start again, and this time it would truly be my own.

Why should I wait? I could leave this moment. Ichiro and Saiko were asleep. Even if they had been awake, how could they stop me? I could drop my burdens here on this riverbank and vanish.

What would Saiko and Ichiro do then? Get lost? Starve? Fall down a mountain? Stumble right into the arms of the soldiers chasing them?

Probably. Why should it worry me?

But it did. I scowled into the darkness, irritated at the sense of responsibility that dragged at my conscience. I owed these two nothing. No debt, no loyalty. And yet I did not like the thought of abandoning them here.

So must I drag them through the wilderness, along miles of roads, over a mountain pass, dodging soldiers and demons all the way? I could hardly bear the thought. I could have covered so much more ground that day, if not for them. I'd be so much safer without them. They could not disappear into a crowd the way I knew how to. They'd draw the soldiers on our trail like bait on a hook.

The darkness between the trees was so tempting. Give me an hour's start, and I'd be gone.

"Please help me. Please . . ."

I leaped to my feet as a girl, younger than Ichiro, crawled sobbing out of the river, dressed in nothing more than rags and her own soaking hair.

"Help me . . ." she begged, reaching out a thin, pale hand. "Please, oh, please . . ."

I left the fire and came closer, but not close enough for that hand to touch me.

She was shivering. Her eyes were huge in her thin face. She struggled feebly to pull herself up the bank, the stones beneath her slick with water and wet moss.

"How did you get into the river?" I asked. I'd heard no splash.

"My mother," she whispered. "She said . . . she said another girl was nothing but a burden. She said better for one to drown than all to starve. Please. Please, I'm so cold. I'm so tired."

The black water lapped hungrily at her knees.

"Get up, then," I told her. "Come to the fire."

"I can't." She held her hand out again. "Have pity. Help me."

I backed up a step. "Get up and walk. I'll help you then."

Her lips pulled back over pointed teeth, and she snarled. Then she lunged at me.

What had once been a shivering girl was scaly skin, black claws, a mouth that gaped wider than a cave. But I let my hand fall from the hilt of my sword, and stood my ground.

The teeth that were bared to devour me, the claws that

were spread to rend the flesh from my bones, swirled into mist and were gone before they touched me.

A ghost. I'd suspected it, and known it when she would not crawl out of the water. She hadn't dared to let me see that she had no feet.

I raised my voice, but not loud enough to wake Ichiro and Saiko.

"Come out," I said. "I know you've been following us."

TWELVE

She came out from the darkness, picking her way over roots and between stones. No ghost, this one. She held up the skirt of her kimono, and her feet in their socks and straw sandals were clearly to be seen.

That kimono was as clean and fresh as snow, patterned with faint gray doves that seemed to take flight at her every movement. Not even the red-gold light of the fire, as she knelt gracefully beside it, could turn the silk anything but white.

"You were watching," I said, and jerked my chin at the river. "Did you set that ghost on me?"

"No."

"But you knew she was there."

"Certainly. She's always somewhere in this river. A sad death, and no one to care for her spirit afterward. She's hungry, the poor little thing. She wants—"

"Wants what?"

Her smile was the only thing about her that was not

beautiful. Too wide. Too many teeth. "What was taken from her in life. A family."

The child's ghost could not have pulled me into the river. But if I'd fallen on the stones trying either to help her or run from her, if I'd hit my head as I slipped under, then perhaps she would've had a sister ghost to keep her company in the cold, black water.

And the pearl? Would it have fallen from my pocket as I drowned? Been carried away in the current and drifted down to the riverbed, to be picked up by—

Who? Ichiro? Saiko? A ghost or a demon? A strange woman in an elegant white kimono, all alone in a wilderness?

"You were in the castle garden," I said, studying her. "You told us the way."

She dipped her head, a graceful nod.

"Why?"

"You know why."

I tightened my hand into a fist, but kept it from sliding inside my jacket to touch the pocket where the jewel lay hidden.

"You don't need to worry." Her smile was smaller now, and without the sight of all those teeth, it looked more normal. "It can't be taken by force. It must be given. You know that?"

"So you think if you help us, I'll give it to you?"

"You may. It's dangerous, after all. It will draw—all sorts of things after you."

"Things like you?"

"Oh, much worse than me." She laughed as she stood,

and the long sleeves and skirts of her kimono danced, the doves fluttering. "Sleep safely tonight. You'll need the rest. Nothing will disturb you. I'll see to that, as long as you are on this side of the mountain. Once you are over the pass, I will not be able to do as much for you."

And she was—

My eyes could not make sense of what was happening to her. All I knew was that, a moment after she had spoken, a white fox sat where she had stood. Its red tongue lolled from its mouth, and its pointed teeth showed in a wide, alarming grin.

It loped toward the forest and melted into the darkness.

* * *

Fox spirits are tricksters; everyone knows that. But this one kept her promise. Nothing else threatened us in the night, though Saiko and Ichiro kept their watches dutifully. When morning came we ate what was left in the pack Masako had filled for us, and went on.

I wouldn't let Ichiro refill our water flasks at the river, but I didn't tell him why.

I led the sister and brother along its bank. The river grew narrower and swifter as we went, burrowing deep into the earth until it became a white snake endlessly racing at the bottom of a gorge. The hour of the hare had just passed when I saw what I had been expecting— a bridge.

It was made of nothing more than cords firmly anchored to trees. Two were at shoulder height and one, between them, at ground level. It spanned the gorge, and its existence was a closely held secret. Every year Madame would send two or three of her girls to cut down the existing bridge and build a new one in a different place. Everyone else in the province had to cross the river at the ford, where it met the road, guarded by Kashihara soldiers who charged Kashihara tolls. But shadow warriors could flit across the river as easily as birds—or tengu—with the help of three sturdy silk cords.

Saiko gasped as a breeze made the bridge dance. "We have to cross *that*?"

"You could swim," I suggested, and she glanced at the river and shuddered, taking a step back. "One at a time, then. The bridge won't take too much weight. I'll go—"

Saiko suddenly fell over.

She hit the ground in a snarl of kimono skirts, thrashing on her back, as a bent sapling beside her whipped upright. Ichiro jumped to her side, but fell also as I kicked his feet out from under him. At the same time, I dropped my pack and dived for the mossy ground.

A knife hummed through the air and buried itself up to the hilt in the soft earth where I had been standing.

I hit the dirt with one shoulder, rolled, and saw in flashes what was happening:

Two figures in mottled, dull-brown clothing, hard to see against a background of branches, dropping out of the trees.

Saiko's blank, shocked face as she quit struggling to stare.

One of the intruders landing next to Ichiro before he could get back to his feet.

The boy, yanked upright, with the bright flash of a blade at his throat.

Then I'd rolled to my feet again and was running full-tilt for the trees, feeling the wind ruffle my hair as another knife missed by a handspan. I was up in the limbs of a giant pine, concealed by thick branches and dull green needles, about ten seconds after Saiko had fallen.

"Can you see where she is?" That was the one who had thrown the knife. A female voice, young but no girl.

"No." That was the one who held Ichiro. A woman. Familiar.

I pressed myself against the trunk, not daring to move as my mind shuffled frantically through options.

I had the advantage of height and, for the moment, secrecy. I knew where they were. They could not be sure where I was. But I'd lose that advantage with the first move I made.

They had the advantage of numbers—two against one. Or perhaps more. There could be others, hidden as I was, in trees or behind boulders, impossible to see until they chose to strike. These were not samurai, boldly swaggering to battle in their bright armor, daring anyone to challenge them. These were shadow warriors, deadly flowers. Ninjas.

Madame's ninjas. Or they wouldn't have known about the bridge, and that I would likely make for it. And Madame had sent not just one, but at least two. She must have wanted us back very badly. Or she wanted the pearl in my pocket.

"Come down," the woman holding Ichiro called. "Or the boy is dead."

The sound of that voice clicked neatly into place in my mind. Instructor Willow.

It was a strange threat for Willow to make. Three nights ago, hadn't I been the one ready to sink a knife into the boy? Why should she think I cared if he died?

But I did care. I'd gotten him away from his uncle's castle, away from Madame's school; I'd kept him safe so far from ghosts and demons, and I didn't plan to lose him to another ninja's blade. It would be such a waste of all my work.

Besides, I didn't believe her.

A small, faintly familiar sound drifted down from the branches above me. I didn't glance up, hoping my enemies had not heard what I had. Instead, I lowered myself onto a new limb, thick and nearly parallel to the ground.

"Kill him," I answered, walking out along the branch I had chosen into their view. I saw Ichiro's eyes widen, but then I saw his face grow trustful. His sister had been right. He trusted much too easily.

I squatted down on my heels and studied the little group—Ichiro tense but calm, Willow holding her knife at his throat, Saiko flat on the ground, the other ninja by her side. She'd stepped on Saiko's long hair, close to the scalp, to keep the girl pinned down and out of her way.

"You're bluffing," the girl holding Saiko told me.

"Maybe you are," I answered, squinting at her face. "Raku? It's you?"

She nodded. I remembered her. She'd been at the school until perhaps four years ago. A good fighter, not the quickest thinker. Slow to react at times.

"Come down, Kata." Willow tightened her grip on Ichiro's shoulder. "You know I won't hesitate."

But she had already hesitated. If Madame had sent her to kill the boy, why hadn't she done so with a thrown knife from the bushes? Why bother setting a snare, unless . . .

Unless Madame had decided that the Kashihara heir would be more valuable alive than dead?

"I'll stay up here, thank you."

"Five seconds, Kata. One . . ."

I heard it again, the sound that had tickled my ear a few moments ago. One little chuckle from a clump of dark needles over my head. And a dozen more to answer it.

"Two . . ."

I twitched my left hand, letting a knife slide into it from the sheath along my forearm. Raku gripped a knife of her own by the blade and cocked it over her shoulder, ready to throw.

"Careful," I warned her. "Madame doesn't want me dead. Or the boy. Does she?"

Slowly, my right hand slid to twist a pinecone loose from a twig near my feet.

"Do you think so? How much are you willing to gamble on that?" Willow's voice was smooth, but I'd seen the frustration that flickered behind her eyes. She *didn't* plan to kill the boy, and she was annoyed that I had guessed.

And she had stopped counting.

"Just this," I answered her, and flicked the pinecone as hard as I could at the branches over my head.

A flurry of black wings and some very inventive cursing exploded out of the bunch of needles. Willow's eyes flew toward the sound, and her blade shifted slightly away from Ichiro's throat and toward this new threat.

Raku's knife flew through the air, but mine met it half-way to the tree, knocking it harmlessly aside, and I dove off the branch to hit the ground close to Willow's feet.

I didn't draw my sword before I leapt—that's a good way to impale yourself—but I turned my body into a weapon, rolling at Ichiro and Willow, thumping into their knees, sending both sprawling.

Ichiro had the sense to scramble out of the way, leaving me free to stamp hard on Willow's wrist as I rolled myself to my feet. I heard bone crack and I snatched her sword from her slack fingers as I continued rising. It was a good thing I did, because Raku was lunging at me, and I barely had a chance to parry a blow that would have split my skull.

Maybe Madame wanted the boy alive, but didn't care quite so much about me . . .

Raku had put all of her weight into that one swing, and now her balance was off, so I dropped the sword and grabbed her wrist and elbow, using her own momentum to heave her over my shoulder. As I did it, my ears caught the sound of running feet. By the time Raku rolled and was up again, I had my own blade out and she was backing away from me.

"Is she gone?" I called, still forcing Raku to retreat toward the river. She had her sword in her hand but did not dare to use it; mine was too close to her throat.

"Yes. She ran," Ichiro confirmed.

Gone didn't mean *defeated*, of course. But Willow prob-ably assumed that Raku would be dead in the next few seconds, and that she herself would be at too much of a disadvantage, facing me alone and with a broken wrist. This was twice I'd taken her sword from her hand. She wouldn't have forgotten that.

Meanwhile, I had the problem of Raku, who had stopped now with her heels an inch from the mossy edge of the gorge.

"You were always quick," she said softly. "And what *was* that in the tree?"

"You wouldn't believe me if I told you," I answered, and she lifted her eyes to mine.

I was hesitating. She knew why.

I'd have to do what I had not done in Ichiro's room. I'd have to kill someone.

Nothing else would work. I could not frighten Raku or threaten her. I could not make a deal with her. I could not tell her I'd spare her life if she'd leave us in peace.

Any deal Raku made with me, she'd ignore. Any promise I forced from her, she'd betray. She would break her word, lie, cheat, steal, do anything necessary to finish what she had begun.

And she knew that I understood.

The honor of a shadow warrior would drive her, the honor of those who were not supposed to have any. A nobleman would laugh at the idea of a ninja with honor. A samurai would spit. They saw us as thieves and greedy cowards, hiding behind disguises, killing in the darkness, selling our skills for gold. They thought we knew nothing of pride or loyalty.

They were wrong.

A ninja's honor meant that she finished her job. A ninja's loyalty, always, was to her mission.

All of these thoughts flashed through my mind in the time it took for Raku's gaze to soften just a little.

"It's your first?" she said too quietly for Saiko and Ichiro to hear. "Do it quickly. Don't think. It will be easier."

She closed her eyes. Her sword hung limply from her slackened fingers.

Now I wasn't the only one hesitating. Everything around me was silent, as if the world had drawn in one huge breath and was waiting to release it.

Then Raku's fingers tightened and her sword flashed up, knocking mine aside. I had to drop to the ground to avoid the tip of her blade as it dove for my eyes. On my knees, I twisted to parry a second, sloppy blow as Raku's foot skidded on a rock covered with wet moss and she fought for her balance, there on the edge.

She didn't see a pale hand reach up from the gorge behind her.

"Help me, please . . ."

Raku whirled. She flinched away from the ghost, tried to recover, and could not. Her sword hit the water a second after she did.

She was swept away by the rushing current. I saw her sleek black head break the surface once before she was pulled under again. The ghost was nowhere to be seen.

"Across the bridge, now!" I shouted, spinning back to look at Saiko and Ichiro. The boy had managed to loosen the cord around Saiko's foot, the one that had been firmly tied to the top of that flexible sapling. When she'd stepped into the loop, she'd knocked aside the peg that had been holding both the cord and the sapling down, and had ended up as helpless as a beetle on its back—just as Raku or Willow had planned.

Brother and sister were both gaping at me.

"Hurry!" I ordered, scanning the undergrowth for signs of Instructor Willow. But it was a different threat that snagged my attention first—a black and buzzing cloud that rose from the pine tree where I had taken shelter. "Get across the bridge *now*." I settled my sword in my hand.

Ichiro waved at Saiko to go first, and stayed at my back as she began to inch her way across. A winged shape detached itself from the dark cloud and darted straight at me.

The tengu pulled itself to a stop and hovered in the air just beyond the reach of my sword. It had human eyes in a beaked face, crowned with an untidy mop of black hair; its body was that of a huge crow, except for the long-fingered hands on the ends of the wings. One of those gripped a sword the length of a chopstick. The other held a pinecone.

I tried to keep my blade between us, but the little creature was as quick as a dragonfly, and tengu were legendary swordsmen. Would I even be able to connect if it decided to attack? And what about the flock overhead, hovering in watchful, waiting silence?

Scowling, the tengu lifted the pinecone and shook its head at me. It had not appreciated being used as a diversion.

I took a risk and sheathed my sword. Then I put my

empty hands together, and bowed in humble apology. Behind me, Ichiro gasped.

The tengu burst into hoarse laughter. I straightened up, and it lobbed the pinecone at my face. Instinctively, I caught it. The tengu wheeled away, joining its flock, and more laughter rained down. So did several more pinecones, bouncing harmlessly off our heads and shoulders as Ichiro and then I crossed the bridge after Saiko.

When I glanced back across the river, the winged black shapes had vanished into the trees once more. But I could feel their sharp eyes watching as I drew my sword, knelt, and sliced through the cords, destroying the bridge for any-one who'd want to follow us.

"But why?" Saiko had collapsed again and was rubbing her ankle gingerly. "That instructor—you defeated her. Surely she won't—"

"Of course she will. She's a *ninja*. They both are." Had Saiko learned nothing at all in her days at the school? "Raku can swim. She may be able to get out of that river, if she doesn't bash her head on a rock. And Willow—I broke her wrist, not her neck. She'll be after us."

"But there's no way across the river, now that the bridge is down. Not unless she goes all the way back to the ford," Ichiro protested.

"She'll *find* one." I groaned. "This is not like a battle—do you understand? We didn't win. They didn't lose. It's not as simple as that. They have a mission to complete, and they will never give up. Our only hope is to make it hard for them to follow us. That means we have to move as quickly as we can."

Speed was the reason I'd reluctantly tossed Willow's sword into the river after Raku's before I'd crossed the bridge. Another blade would have weighed my pack too heavily. Raku's thrown knife had been sacrificed to the river, too, but my own was back in its sheath along my arm.

Saiko let her brother pull her to her feet. "So you should have killed her when you could," she said mildly. She didn't meet my eyes.

"Yes," I said grimly, starting forward along a thin and winding path that led away from the river and into the dense forest all around us. "I should have."

But I hadn't. I hadn't killed Raku any more than I had thrust my knife into Ichiro. Raku and Willow were both ninjas, no doubt. But what was I?

THIRTEEN

Our trail took us up through the woods and, at last, back to a wider road that twisted and wound along a valley floor while mountains rose around us. The rice fields were gone; orchards took their place. The fields grew smaller and stonier. The villages grew shabbier and poorer, and farther apart.

I would not stop and bargain for a midday meal. We were slower than I liked already. Raku might have fished herself out of the water by now, if she had survived. Willow had probably found a way to cross the river, broken wrist and all. And there were other things to worry about in the forest, things deadlier than deadly flowers. Not long ago, I would not have believed that was possible.

Just before the mountain pass that would lead us into Kashihara Yoshisane's country, there was a small village. I was determined to reach it before nightfall. But darkness comes early in the mountains, and the sun was touching the ridge above us when I looked over my shoulder for the hundredth time to see that Saiko was limping and leaning on Ichiro.

I backtracked to meet them. "What is it?"

She gestured at her foot, and I looked down to see her ankle marked with a dark line of bruised flesh where Raku's snare had caught her. The flesh on either side of this line was beginning to swell. My gaze moved to her brother's face. Ichiro's mouth was pinched at the corners, and I could see his eyes aching to close.

I truly hadn't thought it was possible for the two of them to be *slower*. And yet it was.

* * *

"Oh, you poor dear," the headman's wife exclaimed when we knocked on her door. At least I assumed she was the headman's wife. Her house was the largest in the village—two entire rooms—and so we'd headed straight there as the last, lingering bit of the evening's light slipped from the sky.

"Come in, of course, hurry now, and let's get her off that foot," the woman said as we entered. Even as tired as she was, Saiko still managed to slide into a graceful heap on the mats, stained and worn thin with the tracks of many bare feet.

A warlord's daughter had probably never been inside such a humble building in her life. The wooden walls had obvious cracks between the planks, and the air was dim with smoke from the open fire that burned in a square pit dug into the dirt floor. However, if Saiko felt herself too good for such surroundings, she did not reveal it, though she did blink a little as if the smoke stung her eyes.

"Please forgive me for giving you such trouble," she said meekly to our hostess.

I nearly snorted. Trouble for this village wife? What about the trouble she'd been for *me*? I'd practically carried her for the last mile, every step of it uphill.

"Trouble, no such thing," the woman exclaimed. "Travelers often stay here. We're glad enough to have them, for we wouldn't have much news otherwise. Though of course we're poor people here ..." She was wrapping a damp, mostly clean rag around Saiko's foot, as she let her sentence trail off, expectantly.

I'd reluctantly agreed to give up the last of our copper coins for meals and bedding, when the doorway darkened. I looked up, trying to slip my hand toward one of my throwing knives without being too obvious about it. But our hostess's glad cry was reassuring.

"*There* you are, Ryoichi! Tell me you've brought something for the pot. For look, visitors! The first in, oh, well. Tell me, you killed something? Didn't you?"

The man at the door ducked his head to come in and revealed himself to be much younger than I'd thought at first.

"Here, Mother." He handed her three or four good-sized fish hanging from a forked stick threaded through their gills. So she was the headman's mother, not his wife. She kissed his cheek in delight and set about scaling and cleaning his catch, while the young man came and sat by the fire.

"Don't you worry, we'll have something for you in a heartbeat; nothing makes you hungrier than traveling," the woman chattered as she worked. "You must tell us, where are you headed? We know all the best roads, of course."

I nodded at Saiko to do the talking. Perhaps it wasn't wise; I shouldn't let her draw more attention to herself than she could help. But lies sounded better coming out of her mouth. No one was inclined to disbelieve that face.

Besides, somehow, my eyes wanted to rest on the young man beside the fire.

Perhaps he was five or six years older than I was. His mother had called him Ryoichi, hadn't she? The firelight turned his skin bronze and stroked the smooth planes under his cheekbones. He was smiling faintly as his mother talked, but he didn't seem to be listening closely. There was something on his mind, and I found myself wondering what it was.

My thoughts, and the young man's, too, were interrupted by his mother's gasp of horror.

"Oh, no, you can't go *that* way!"

I looked up as Saiko, confused, stopped speaking. Ichiro, yawning in a corner, was no help to anybody.

"I was just telling our hostess that we're headed over the mountains," Saiko said apologetically, as though our travel plans might have caused offense.

"Oh, no, no, never. Ryoichi, aren't I right? Such nice young people, all on their own, too. We can't let anything happen to them. Ryoichi, tell them!"

"The pass?" Ryoichi was frowning. "No, my mother is right. It's not safe."

"Rock falls?" I asked.

"Bandits."

A pack of thieves, it seemed, had moved into a cave a few months ago and had been preying on travelers ever since.

"They have swords," Ryoichi said, frowning at the fire. "Bows. Fine weapons. They must be ronin. Perhaps their warlord died, and they decided he wasn't worth avenging."

Saiko looked scandalized. Unlike ninjas, hired by anyone who could pay them, a samurai should follow a single master all his life. If one did happen, through ill luck or poor planning, to outlive his lord, the correct response was either a sword through the stomach or an existence devoted to vengeance. Certainly not a choice to sell his fighting skills or use them to take whatever he wanted.

"What about your own lord?" I asked. "Why hasn't he driven these bandits away?"

"We have no lord," Ryoichi answered.

"You're a free village?" Startled, I looked at him closely.

"You belong to no one?" Saiko looked more scandalized than ever. If it was distasteful for a samurai to live with no lord, it was appalling for peasants to do so.

"We live between two Kashiharas," Ryoichi said. "And each one needs us." His back straightened a little with pride. "It's very difficult—in fact, it's impossible—to find the way through the pass between their territories without a guide who's known the mountains since childhood."

Impossible? Maybe for most travelers. But most travelers did not have the advantage of untold hours spent studying Madame Chiyome's maps.

"Those two lords might have fought over this village like

two dogs over a bone," Ryoichi went on. Ichiro squirmed until Saiko flicked him a glance. "But my father—he was the headman before me—offered them a different solution. We serve both and neither. We give free passage to anyone who wears the Kashihara dragonfly. Then there is no way one brother can hold the pass for himself and keep the other out. In return, they leave us in peace."

That headman had been a clever man to come up with that plan, I thought, and bold as well, to propose it to not one but two warlords who both had the power to cut off his head and hang it from their castle walls for insolence if they'd been so inclined.

"We've lived free since that day," Ryoichi went on. "We obey no master. We belong to ourselves."

Saiko smoothed her hands over her skirt, tucking it under her knees. Her face was a well-bred blank.

"But who protects you?" Ichiro asked, fully awake now and leaning forward with concern. "If another warlord comes with an army? Or thieves, or men like those bandits?"

"The mountains protect us," Ryoichi said quietly. "We know where to hide if we must. And we protect one another." He sighed. "Or we have until now."

"Those bandits don't trouble us," his mother put in. "We're too poor for them to bother with, I suppose. But the travelers . . . they've all but stopped coming. You're the first we've seen in weeks. We can grow our own vegetables and catch our own fish. For some things we need money, though. We can't grow rice up here, or millet, either. Shizuko's little boy is ailing, and the doctor won't take what we can trade. And priests need paying for the rituals they do. Still, our troubles aren't yours, are they? Come, the meal is ready."

She filled our bowls and the three of us shoveled hot, flaky white fish into our mouths. Saiko coughed the bones delicately into her hand. I spat mine directly into the fire.

"You need to hire someone," I said, holding my bowl out for Ryoichi's mother to spoon hot broth into it. "To fight those bandits off."

Ryoichi snorted. "The whole village together doesn't have the coins to pay a single soldier, much less a band of them. These days, there are enough battles to keep every warrior in the land busy. Why should they fight for what we can afford to pay?"

"Not a warrior," I answered him with a shake of my head. "You need a ninja."

And that was why, the next night, I lay flat on my face in sparse grass, most of the way up a mountain.

I'd been waiting here while the sun slid down the western sky. Now the remaining light was dim and shadowy enough that I dared ease myself forward to peer over the edge of a steep drop.

Below me was the mouth of a cave, with a small plateau before it. Beyond the flat area, the land dropped again down to a ravine with an icy creek tumbling along its bottom. Downstream, the ravine gradually widened and flattened until it reached a valley where the shoulders of two mountains leaned together. Between those shoulders was the pass that led into Lord Yoshisane's territory.

Travelers who wanted to reach that pass would be in full view of anyone watching from the mouth of the cave. Which was why the bandits had chosen it to live in.

Perhaps thirty feet below me, one of the bandits was crouched, keeping an eye on everything below him. Fortunately, he did not think of looking up, and I was careful to give him no reason to, letting the stillness of the stones around me soak into my muscles and bones. I kept my ears alert, though, and not only for sounds from the cave. How many bakemono did this mountain hide, buried in deep caves, lurking in hidden pools, drifting without form or shape in the cold mists that clung to the highest peaks? How many of them might be stirred to wakefulness and hunger by the pearl in my pocket? The white fox had said she could offer us some protection, as long as we were on this side of the pass. But could she save us from every demon? Could I even count on her to try?

Trust no ally for more than you've paid him. Or, in this case, her.

And demons were not the only threats. Where was Willow? And was she the only ninja on our trail? I had to hope so, which meant I had to hope that Raku had drowned. It was obviously better to have one shadow warrior tracking us than two.

So it was odd, that little flutter of hope that dwelled inside my ribcage. I hadn't seen Raku's body, after all. Maybe she was injured, but not dead. Maybe she'd crawled out of the water far enough downstream to be no real threat to us as long as we kept moving. Maybe . . .

Maybe I should keep my mind on my mission.

At the moment, at least, my ears heard no sound of pursuit, human or otherwise. The man outside the cave stood, shifted his weight from foot to foot, and turned his head, letting his gaze move steadily back and forth over the terrain.

Then something new came to my ears, faint and distant: running feet, sandals slapping on stone. The bandit on guard snatched a bow from his shoulder, pulling a bamboo arrow from a quiver and fitting it quickly and expertly into place.

Below him, a man broke free of the tree line and headed up the slope toward the creek bed. He paused briefly, holding out his hands to show that he was unarmed. Then he resumed his steady jog, as if he had no time to waste.

The guard called out, and two more men came out of the cave behind him. I squinted in the growing dark to see them more clearly. Ronin beyond a doubt. Their armor, once fine, was dented and scratched, the lacquer chipped off the metal plates. Their hair was unkempt, loosed from the neat topknots that showed a samurai's rank, and one had so far forgotten his dignity as to let a beard cover his chin. But each wore two swords through his belt, and each stood like a fighter, easy on his feet, alert, strong.

While the first guard kept his arrow aimed at the approaching stranger, the two newcomers started off down the slope toward him. They met the running man where the creek spread out into a dozen rivulets across the flatter ground. One of the ronin drew his longer sword. The other simply stood with crossed arms, listening. I could not hear the words they traded, but I could see their reactions. The one with the drawn sword grabbed the intruder by the scruff of his neck and thrust him uphill toward the cave. Soon they were close enough for me to recognize Ryoichi's face.

I had my own sword at my belt, but it would be little use from where I lay. Both knives were in their sheaths along my forearms. I'd never promised Ryoichi I'd come to his aid if things went wrong, but I found myself calculating distances and chances. Two knives. Three men. Very little hope that I'd be able to do much if the young village head-man proved to be a poor actor or if the bandits were more clever, or less cowardly, than I'd hoped.

A fourth man stepped out of the cave. The bandit hold-ing Ryoichi pushed him forward. The way they all looked at the new arrival confirmed what I'd guessed—he was their leader.

Darkness was falling—no, not falling. Up here, in this land of stones and sky, the darkness seem to rise instead, as if it were leaking out from every crack and hollow. I couldn't clearly see the details of the little gathering below me, but I could sense how the men stood: the upright confidence of the bandit leader, the way Ryoichi leaned forward, his shoulders hunched, his hands making quick, tight gestures. He looked nervous. He looked worried. He looked fearful.

Good. He was supposed to.

Ryoichi flung out one arm, gesturing toward the ravine below, the thick line of trees, the way down to his village.

I was careful not to hold my breath, but my fingers tightened in the short, tough grass until I found I'd pulled a handful up by its roots. Which was careless. Suppose I accidentally loosed a little shower of dirt over the edge and one of the men below glanced up? Suppose they spotted me?

They'd slit Ryoichi's throat first, and I'd be next. And on top of that, my plan would be a failure. I forced my fingers to relax.

The bandit leader had turned his head to follow Ryoichi's gesture. He nodded. Then he reached into a silk pouch hanging at his belt and flipped something small and round through the air toward Ryoichi.

Ryoichi caught the coin, glanced at it, lifted his chin, and tossed it back.

My gut clenched. That had *not* been part of my plan. How would the bandit react? Would he be startled? Would he begin to think more carefully about who Ryoichi was and what he had said? Why hadn't that fool of a headman simply snatched the coin in gleeful gratitude and run?

Ryoichi spoke a few short words. My whole plan hung in the balance, success or failure depending on a conversation I could not hear.

Then the headman began to jog lightly and quickly down the slope, surefooted even in the gathering dusk. The three bandits before the cave turned to their leader, but all his attention was focused on the flickers of warm yellow light that, far below, were beginning to shine through the trees.

Close to Ryoichi's village, something was moving. In the darkness, a darker line stretched across the slope of the mountain, visible only here and there where it moved between stands of trees or clumps of brush. The head of the line broke free from a copse of pine and a figure on horseback could be glimpsed in the glow of the torches carried by two men on foot. There was a flash of bulky red armor, a helmet crowned with horns.

It appeared that a troop of soldiers had come to rout troublesome bandits out of their mountain pass. A *large* troop of soldiers with a samurai at their head.

The bandit leader shouted, the cave behind him burst into frantic activity, and I began to crawl backward. Once I could move without being seen, I followed the trail Ryoichi had marked for me when he guided me up. Each time I passed one of his signals—a stone balanced on another, three sticks laid to form an arrow—I kicked them apart, leaving no sign that either of us had been here.

I slipped over a ridge and down its other side, and then I could move more freely, cut off from the vision of anyone who might be watching from the cave's mouth. At last I worked myself down to the lower slopes and the cover of the tree line. Then I paused in the ink-black shadow of an ancient cedar, waiting to let the line of advancing troops make their way up to me.

They'd been toiling slowly up the mountainside, as heavily armed men would, of course, toil, allowing the bandits time to empty their cave and move on. The ronin wouldn't head over the mountain pass, since that would be too close to their enemy, but they'd be fools if they hadn't mapped out another escape route, or two, or three.

I stepped from the shadow of my tree in front of the mounted leader, holding up one hand.

"Kata!" Ichiro cried, stopping in his tracks.

I took a few quick steps and caught hold of his stirrup. "Don't *shout!*" I ordered, keeping my voice low. "And don't stop. Keep the horse moving."

Ichiro's eyes, excited and anxious, peered down at me from the depths of his oversized helmet. "Did it work?" he asked.

I nodded, and the boy nudged his mount, a good-natured and skinny wreck of a beast owned by all the villagers together. The animal heaved itself into a shambling walk once more. I kept pace alongside. "It's going well," I told him. "They were clearing out of the cave when I left. Keep moving, but go slowly. Don't leave the forest. When you reach the end of the tree line, stop there and wait for me." I stepped back into the shadows to let Ichiro and his followers pass.

We'd cobbled the boy's outfit together overnight, using every scrap of red cloth that the village possessed, padding his jacket and trousers with straw to make him seem bigger than he was. The helmet had been carved out of bark and glued together with pine pitch, topped with a pair of horns that were actually twisted tree roots. One good clout would have knocked the thing to pieces, but from a distance on a dark night, glimpsed by torchlight, it looked just enough like something a samurai might wear into battle to terrify his enemies.

The villagers trailing behind Ichiro were dressed in their darkest clothes, some with furs or quilts over their shoulders to make them look as bulky as armored warriors, most with cooking pots on their heads to pass for helmets. The hunters carried their own bows and had quivers on their backs. We'd pulled the blades off hoes and sharpened the sticks into points so that they'd look like spears, and used broad leaves to imitate naginata, the long poles topped by heavy, curved blades.

Old grannies and aunties hobbled determinedly along, grandfathers marched behind them, girls dressed in their brothers' clothes kept pace, boys jumped out of their skins with the thrill. I spotted Ryoichi's face under a cooking pot as he passed, his hand under his mother's elbow, helping her along. Even Saiko, her foot much improved by a night of rest, had a pair of trousers on and an old rake in her hand.

There couldn't have been more than forty of them, all told, but every time they passed behind a thick clump of trees or a rocky outcrop, some of those in front would douse their torches and sprint to the back of the line, there to light them again. It would be hard, I hoped, for the bandits to guess the true numbers of such a confused and straggling procession.

I turned back the way I'd come. If I returned to the ridge I'd crossed earlier, I'd be able to get another glimpse of the cave, to be sure the bandits had not left a rearguard or lingered to pack stolen treasure. It wouldn't do to let Ichiro and his ragtag army of children and grandmothers, not to mention his useless sister, come across any real threat.

Then something thick and black and heavy came down over my head, smothering my scream, and I was dragged into the undergrowth so quickly and deftly that, if Ichiro or Ryoichi or any of their band had looked back, they would have noticed nothing.

I had vanished as quickly and utterly as if a ghost had stolen me.

FOURTEEN

The bag was pulled off my head and I gasped in fresh air, blinked, and tried to get my eyes to make sense out of what I was seeing.

I'd fought as hard as I could, but it had been no use. Nothing in my training had prepared me to face a half a dozen hardened warriors who were mostly trying to sit on me. I knew several of them would be bruised or bleeding, but in the end they'd gotten ropes on me, kept me bundled in the sack, carried me a good distance uphill, and dumped me here.

For half a moment I saw only blotches of shadow and blurs of red-orange light. Then my eyes adjusted, and I realized I was lying on the floor of a cave, with my face against muddy rock.

A man was kneeling at the cave's mouth, blowing hard on a few wisps of flame that curled around tiny twigs. As the flames caught, he sat up and began feeding the fire larger sticks. Where the light could reach, all was golden. But back where I had been dropped, the darkness was deep.

Men were walking into the cave with sacks, bundles, and weapons, finding places to stack them. One was unrolling a sleeping mat. No one seemed to be making frantic preparations to depart.

One of the bandits knelt to check that my wrists were still securely tied behind my back and then pulled loose the gag that had been shoved into my mouth. He gave a tug to the cords around my ankles as well.

All this was done as efficiently and unemotionally as a man checking his horse's harness. He didn't hate me, and he didn't pity me; he just wanted to be sure I wasn't going anywhere.

He rose and walked off, waving at someone as he went.

I wriggled myself up to a sitting position and began to work on the rope around my hands. It wouldn't take me too long, but I needed to be subtle. No sense in letting these bandits know I was free until I decided to use that freedom.

They'd taken my sandals when they'd first tied my feet. I could manage without; I'd run barefoot over sharp gravel and bits of broken pottery before. But turning an ankle or breaking a toe on a rocky mountain slope would slow me down considerably. If I planned carefully, maybe I could find a new pair of shoes before I escaped.

Which I must do soon. My plan had fallen apart; the bandits had not been fooled. I could curse myself later for overconfidence or stupidity or whatever had made me fail, but right now I needed freedom, and not just for myself.

Ichiro. Saiko. Ryoichi and his mother and all of his villagers. I'd played with their lives too blithely and now they were in danger. These bandits were not likely to take kindly to our attempts to scare them out of their comfortable cave. I had to warn the others—or, if I was too late for that, defend them.

At the moment, though, I could not even defend myself. A man was coming toward me, and my hands were only half-free.

The firelight was behind him, and so he loomed like a bat, the sleeves of his short kimono flapping as if ready for flight. He crouched out of reach of my feet should I try to kick, and set something down on the stone floor with a clink.

Metal rubbed on metal as he turned the shield of a dark lantern to let a sliver of light beam out of the darkness and onto my face.

"That's better," said a voice I recognized. "I wanted to see you clearly—the girl who nearly sent every single one of my warriors running for the next province."

He said this last part loudly enough for several men nearby to hear, and there were groans and some embarrassed laughter.

"Your little performance was quite convincing," the bandit leader went on. "From a distance, at least. If I hadn't decided to take a few men and get a closer look at our enemy—it was so hard to figure out just how many there were—I would never have known we were facing a terrifying troop of grandmothers and aunties waving hoes and pitchforks, taking their orders from a half-grown girl." He leaned a little closer. "You think yourself very clever?"

One loop of cord slipped over the mound of muscle where my right thumb joined the hand. That should make the rest easier. But it was slow work. I had to keep my shoulders still, not to let him guess what I was doing.

"You and your friends were laughing at us?"

They'd taken my sword, of course, and the knives that had been hidden up my sleeves. But it had been dark and there hadn't been time to search me properly. I had other weapons, if only I could get to them.

"You think you've made fools of us?"

A sound caught my ear, softer than his voice, softer than the hiss and crackle of the fire behind him—the silky whisper of a sharp and well-oiled blade sliding slowly from its sheath.

"And I say . . ."

I braced myself, watching that dark figure for a sign that he was about to pounce. My hands were not quite free. If he moved, I'd need to use my feet. Just because my ankles were tied didn't mean I was helpless. One quick kick to the chest with both feet together, or better yet, the jaw or the bridge of the nose . . .

"You're right!"

He slapped the lantern open wider, so that the light fell on his face as well as my own, and his teeth flashed white under his moustache as he laughed.

Other men were laughing, too, at his words and at the bare shock on my face.

"We were ready to scamper across the mountains with

only what we could carry. You came within a heartbeat of making men who've spent their lives in battle flee like frightened rabbits."

I was impressed by how deftly the bandit knocked aside the sandal that came flying out of the darkness at his head, without ever taking his eyes off me.

"But I decided I didn't want to leave without a chance to speak with you, girl." He grinned even more widely, and in one quick motion, used the dagger in his hand to slash the cords that held my ankles together. "I could tell you were working on your hands. Got them free yet? Yes, I see you do. Let's be comfortable and chat. I have a few things to say to you."

Moments later I found myself kneeling by the fire, a haunch of roasted rabbit in one hand and a cup of warm rice wine in the other.

Relief is a weakness; it reveals that you were frightened. So I tried not to show any. But I wasn't sure I was succeeding.

This leader of bandits wasn't going to take his vengeance on me or on Ryoichi's villagers? He wasn't angry at our deception? He wanted to . . . talk?

"So the villagers hired you?" he asked cordially, squatting beside me. "I'm surprised they could afford an agent of your quality."

I took a hasty bite of greasy meat as an excuse to turn my face away. An agent of my quality? After my plan had failed miserably and I'd let myself be captured like the rawest recruit?

"I won't ask what they paid you," the bandit went on,

"but I'll see they get their money's worth. We'll be on our way. To tell you the truth, I already thought we'd been in this spot long enough. Life can't be easy for that little village with the likes of us camped up here." I cast a sidelong glance in his direction. He looked as if he meant what he said. "After all, as your friend said when he tossed my coin back at me—one free man should do a service for another when he can."

There were a few grumbles from the others around the fire as his men began to realize that he was ordering them to repack what they had just started to unpack. The captain raised his voice. "And these ruffians will do as I say, unless any of them wants to challenge me for the leadership."

The man on my other side, a hulk as wide as a mountain with a face scarred from eyebrow to chin, snorted as he rolled a sleeping mat out across the ground. "Not likely, Commander Otani. We remember the last man who tried it."

"Ah, yes. Where *is* his head, again?"

Otani seemed to think that was a joke. Not all of his men were smiling.

"But before we pack up, a question or two. First, *can* you speak? You have a tongue in that clever head?"

I nodded.

He groaned. "Not quite what I was hoping for. Let's try again. Maybe a different question—I have it! What's your name?"

Silence is your best ally. Silence and darkness.

I'd been quiet all of this time partly because of surprise. I'd expected several things when I was carried, bound, into a bandit's cave. Friendly chatter hadn't been one of them.

You are a shadow, a ghost. No one knows you. Secrecy is your armor.

It wasn't much of a name, or an identity. Just the single word. Even in the days when I'd had a family, none of us had been noble or wealthy or powerful enough to put a family name before a personal one.

Now, of course, I had no family. No village. No one to serve and no one who served me. I did not even have the school anymore. I had nothing that was truly mine besides my scrap of a name and the pearl in my pocket.

So I was not about to hand that name to my kidnapper, this bewildering man who seemed as likely to talk me to death as he did to cut my throat.

"No? I don't usually do so poorly, conversing with a lady." Otani tipped his head to one side and studied me thoughtfully through narrowed eyes. "Did I kidnap the wrong one, perhaps? Were you just following orders, my sweet? Should I be talking to that boy on the horse? Was *he* the brains behind your plan?"

"No," I growled, and he laughed.

"So it's pride that loosens your tongue. I should have guessed. Well, excellent. It's your pride that I plan to appeal to. No need to put that suspicious look on your face. I may not be an honest man, but I am an honorable one. Does anyone here say differently?"

There was another stern look around the fire and much hasty shaking of heads.

"Good, then. I'll put an honorable proposal to you. Would you like to join us?"

I stared.

"Oh, don't turn mute again. Which part didn't you understand?"

"Join you?" I asked, a little hoarse with surprise. It wasn't good, the way this man could keep me off balance. *Never let yourself be surprised. Anticipate every move your enemy might make.*

But was this man telling me that he was not my enemy?

I forced myself to speak more, letting my lip curl with distaste. "Join you as . . . what? I'm no . . ." No courtesan, concubine, prostitute. If that's what he thought he'd kidnapped, he'd be sorry he'd left my hands free.

Otani snorted. "I don't need any more of those." His men laughed again. "No, that's not what I meant. As a ninja, of course. That's what you are."

Not much point to denying it now. I felt my spine straightening a little. "You want to hire me?" This might be useful. Ryoichi's villagers could not pay me much. This bandit, on the other hand—what kind of stolen treasure did his cave hold?

"Well, not quite. Not exactly. I want you to work for me, yes. But not to complete one mission and then vanish into the night. I want you to ride with us." He leaned forward, serious now, and I saw the leader that hid behind the jokes and the chatter, the one his men had followed into battle and then into outlawry. "Your little ruse was clever. It was more than clever. I could use that kind of thinking. You'd be a member of my band. A share of whatever we take would be yours."

"Whatever you steal," I corrected.

"You're in the wrong profession, little one, if stealing bothers you. What do you say?"

I shook my head. "I—no. I'm not—I work alone. I have to."

"Always? Forever?" He looked as if he knew me. I resented it. "Think about it, girl with no name. You'd have comrades. Someone to talk to. Someone at your back in battle. Someone to bury you when your luck runs out." The faces of his men were somber in the shifting firelight. "In these days, that may be the most anyone can hope for."

Trust no friend farther than you can see her. Trust no ally for more than you've paid him.

"Think about it." Otani was back on his feet. "We'll finish packing up and leave at dawn. You can come with us if you want. If not, you can go." My eyes lifted to his face, and he seemed to read the question there. "My word on it, girl with no name. You are free to choose."

Free?

The men around me sighed and grumbled and busied themselves gathering gear and weapons and foodstuff into packs for the second time that night. Since I had nothing to pack, I stayed beside the fire with my cup of rice wine untouched in my hands.

I should leave. Otani had said I could do so; I should take him at his word. Ichiro and Ryoichi and their mock army were waiting for me.

Yet I didn't go. I took a slow sip of my drink, but no more. I needed a clear head.

Free to choose.

I had been thinking of freedom as something the pearl could buy for me. Now someone was simply offering it to me. As though it were mine for the taking.

I shook my head a little, as if that would settle my thoughts into place. Then I set my cup down and rose. Otani was kneeling by a pack, sorting through its contents. He dumped a pair of sandals, a bundle of salted plums, and a small, heavy sack onto the floor of the cave. The knot that held the sack shut had been tied carelessly, and it slipped loose. Gold coins rolled and bounced around our feet.

"I packed in a bit of a hurry," Otani said, pausing in his collection of errant coins to look up at me. "So you've decided?"

I nodded. Then I shook my head.

He quirked an eyebrow. "I think you will actually have to open your mouth to make your answer clear."

"No."

He seemed to be waiting for more. I crouched down so I could speak to him on his level.

"My . . . friends." It was an odd word, and not the right one. Saiko and Ichiro were hardly friends. I'd known him only a few days, her barely longer. I didn't trust them. I didn't like them. Well, the boy, perhaps. He was hard to dislike. But he was Saiko's brother. And when I thought of her—

She'd worn a cooking pot on her head tonight, and abandoned her dignity as a warlord's daughter far enough to march beside Ryoichi's villagers. It had been her quick fingers that had sewn most of Ichiro's make-believe armor.

I might be ready to concede that she was not entirely useless.

But liking her—that was not even a possibility.

Still, I was on a mission with the two of them. I could not abandon it halfway.

"There is something I must finish," I said finally.

"With your . . ." Otani paused. "Friends."

I looked squarely into those eyes that seemed to know too much about me. "Yes."

I had a sharp steel rod sewn into my sleeve, long enough to reach a man's heart. I had a cord around my waist that could go around his throat, and the small but deadly blade inside my hairpin. And of course I had my own two hands. All of them could be lethal if he did not like to have his offer refused.

He shrugged. "Loyalty is an admirable quality, my dear. It rarely works to interfere with it. Consider the offer open." He went back to organizing his pack. "You can find us if you want to, I imagine, once you're done with, well, whatever it is you're doing."

They gave me back my weapons and my sandals and let me go.

Still more than a little astonished, I paused outside the cave and waited for my eyes to adjust to the moonlight before I began to ease my way down the slope. A flash of white to one side made my heart beat quicker, and when I turned my head I saw the white fox sitting on top of a rock her own height. The minute I saw her, she jumped down and vanished behind a larger stone.

Poets always describe moonlight as silver, but I could never see it as anything but gray. The mountains rising around me were black masses against a sky spattered with white stars. I could vaguely see the pass below me, and below it, the forest, a warm and living dark against the dry, cool dark of stone. In that darkness, I could spot wavering flashes of warm yellow light.

I headed downhill, toward the lights. Before I reached them, they began to come slowly up the slope toward me.

What was Ryoichi doing? Or was this Ichiro's idea? Why didn't the boy stay in the trees as I'd told him to? I hoped the child wasn't starting to get his own ideas as to how a mission should be handled. That would never do.

As I got closer, voices rose to meet me.

"But they're bandits. They're armed."

"What are we going to *do*, exactly, up there at that cave?"

"I don't know yet." That voice I recognized. It was Ryoichi's.

"Well, that's an excellent plan," someone grumbled.

"We can't simply leave her." That was Ichiro. "If they caught her, we have to do *something*."

"We must know what's become of her!" Saiko sounded unexpectedly fierce.

When I realized what they were doing, I was so surprised I was robbed of speech for the second time that night.

They were coming to rescue me.

I had not expected anything of the sort. Neither had I expected the look of joy on Ichiro's face as I stepped into the torchlight and he flung himself off his swaybacked horse and dashed to throw his arms around me.

Then they were all crowding near, exclaiming and marveling, patting my back and shaking their heads and asking questions and not listening to the answers and cheering when I told them the bandits were leaving, and laughing even though no joke had been made. When you set out bravely and anxiously to fight ruthless armed bandits and discover that you don't have to, you don't need a joke to laugh.

In all of the talk I did not quite manage to correct their assumption that I had escaped.

And why should I, after all? Better to let them think no ninja could be held for long. Better to let them imagine that ropes and locks and chains were as frail as mist or as weak as cobwebs to a shadow warrior. The more people who thought that, the easier every ninja's job was.

Somehow, though, the sight of Ryoichi's admiring grin made a ticklish and uncomfortable feeling squirm under my ribs. I wished I could tell him the truth about what had happened.

But I couldn't. Or I didn't, not even when we'd gone back to the village for what was left of the night, not even when morning came. It was time to move on.

FIFTEEN

We couldn't stay, though Ryoichi's mother and many others pressed us to spend one more night, eat their food, drink their carefully hoarded rice wine. But we had no time to spare. If I was ever to finish this mission, we had to keep moving. It was the only way Ichiro and Saiko would be safe, and I would finally be free.

Free to find Otani and his ronin again? Free to set out into the world on my own with the pearl?

I didn't know. I wasn't sure. But I did know we had to leave. There was at least one ninja on our trail, and demons as well, and these villagers had been kind.

It felt odd to think of it. Kindness was not something I had been taught to expect from an employer.

You finished the mission. You collected your fee. You expected your client to treat you with disdain, and you made sure no one guessed that he'd hired a ninja to do work a man with honor would not stoop to.

But Ryoichi's villagers—they praised me, and thanked me, and piled in my hands all the copper coins they could spare, and some they probably couldn't. One old woman even kissed me. And they'd been prepared to tackle bandits for my sake, armed with nothing more than hunters' bows and farmers' tools.

It left me feeling startled, and unsettled, and even more eager to be on our way.

The pass, now free of bandits, was not difficult to cross with Ryoichi's guidance. But once he turned back, we found that the trail had a perverse mind of its own. It took us across a series of ravines, every downward slope slippery and rocky, every uphill stretch torturous. I didn't let Saiko and Ichiro stop to rest, I barely let them stop to eat, and I didn't tell them why. The fox had warned me that she could give us little protection once we were on the other side of the mountain. We'd need a shelter of some kind before nightfall.

Scrambling up a slope ahead of me, Ichiro kicked a rock loose. It rolled and bounced downhill to hit me squarely in the knee, leaving a tight ball of pain clustered around the joint. It didn't matter. Keep going.

Blisters on my feet; dust and grit in my eyes, in my hair, and on my tongue; skin scraped off my hands. None of it mattered. Keep going.

When Saiko began to limp again, I bandaged her foot tightly with damp cotton strips. When Ichiro complained that he was hungry, I told him to fill his stomach with water at every creek we passed. I growled at them. I glared at them. I all but pushed Saiko up the steeper slopes.

But I did not tell them what I could hear behind us.

We were being tracked. The sound was like an echo. When we stopped, it stopped. But sometimes my ears could catch a footfall, soft but heavy, gentle as a cat's, not too far away.

Perhaps Willow had found us. Perhaps something worse had done so. I couldn't tell. Keep going.

When the light slanting through leaves and pine needles turned a rich amber, we paused on top of a ridge of old, crumbling stone. "There. See that?" I pointed.

Saiko, looking almost not pretty, was slumped on a tree root. Ichiro obediently turned his gaze in the direction of my finger. "What?"

"The road. See?"

"*That* far?"

I'd thought the sight of the narrow brown ribbon below, following the path of a silvery-gray river, would lift their spirits. I'd been mistaken.

"It's not so far," I said, a little helplessly. At the school there had been punishments in plenty for a girl who thought she could give in to exhaustion. But it wasn't as if I had a bamboo rod handy to beat these two into motion, so I had to try encouragement instead. I wasn't very good at it. "Look. See the bridge? There's a temple on the other side of the river. We'll be safe there for the night."

"We can't," Ichiro said. "Kata, we can't make it all that way before dark."

And he was right. They couldn't.

I took a second look at the temple below. I *might* be able to reach it before the sun was entirely gone. These two would not. I turned to scan our surroundings.

"You don't have to," I told Ichiro.

Where we stood, the path split. One branch led downhill, a narrow, steep, rocky nightmare of a track, best suited to goats. But the other followed the backbone of the ridge, an easier walk, before it took a hitch between two cedars and vanished into the gathering darkness.

And in that gathering darkness, I'd seen light.

Pale and steady—it wasn't a campfire or a torch. Someone behind a paper screen had lit an oil lamp.

The path took us through so many twists and turns I had trouble keeping track of our direction, and I never was quite sure how long we'd followed it. But I did not once lose sight of that light, and at last the trail decanted us into a small clearing. Ichiro tripped over a root and sat down. I paused to take in what I saw.

It wasn't a warlord's mansion. But it wasn't a peasant's hut, either. A curving path of smooth white stones began at our feet and led to a tidy farmhouse, large enough for more than one room inside, with a flowering plum by the door, its pale and delicate blossoms like tiny moons against its small, dark leaves.

A door slid back, and someone looked out.

"What's that—oh, my. Are you lost?" A woman, neither old nor young, was in the doorway. Her face was worried and kind.

"All alone? And out at night? Come in. Come in."

Ichiro had struggled back to his feet. Saiko glanced questioningly at me.

The woman looked harmless enough. Still, it was an odd place for a farmhouse. No fields or orchards surrounded it. No other dwellings were nearby.

But we had no choice. The dark was swooping in, closing like wings around us. And the dark held whatever it was that had been following us for hours. "A night's lodgings, mistress?" I asked. "We can pay."

"You poor things," she said kindly. "Of course you can stay the night. I wouldn't dream of taking payment from guests. Just come in."

A few minutes later we were seated by her hearth. The first thing our hostess did was to lock the window shutters. The next was to brew tea.

She poured herself a cup from the same pot, and sipped it. So I put mine to my lips. It was good, hot and fresh, with no bitter aftertaste. It smelled like the tea Madame kept for her richest clients.

I noticed a white vase with a spray of plum blossom in a niche on the wall. Fresh, clean mats on the floor, soft and thick under our knees. The sway and drape of the woman's kimono as she knelt to pour the tea, deftly catching the swinging sleeve and tucking it out of her way—it was a deep plum color with simple embroidery, but it was still silk, and not cheap silk either. Her hair, glossy with camellia oil, was piled high on her head, leaving the back of her neck bare.

This was no isolated farmhouse. She was no farmer's wife.

In fact, she was no one's wife.

"The tea, how is it? Warming you up a little?" she asked.

"Are you all alone here, Mistress . . . ?" I prodded gently.

"Okui." She smiled, perfectly. She'd practiced; I could tell. "And I'm not always on my own. Servants, of course. And I have visitors now and then. One in particular."

I felt myself relaxing, just a little.

Courtesan and ninja—we are not that far apart. No warlord likes to admit that they employ either one of us, but they all do.

If Okui's employer preferred to keep her in an elegant little house on a mountainside, well, perhaps that was more convenient and less risky than visiting the pleasure quarters of a city, where there might be many dangers, and many witnesses.

A door slid open to show a skinny young girl on her knees. With her face hidden behind her hair, she picked up the tray she had set down beside her and rose to her feet. Other servants followed her, and the smells made me dizzy. Steaming soup, hot rice, sliced fish, cakes that had been fried crisp and others stuffed with tender, savory meat. Dried melon. Pickled plums. Tiny oranges that looked ready to burst with juice.

Okui's employer was a wealthy man, clearly, and he must have liked his food.

I caught Saiko's eye. "Perhaps we could wash first?" I suggested.

"Oh, don't bother with such formality!" Okui laughed. "As hungry as this poor boy looks, it would be cruel to keep him from his dinner another moment." And before I could say another word, Ichiro had a soft, pink hunk of salmon in his mouth.

"Aren't you hungry, Mistress Okui?" he asked, swallowing quickly to make room for more.

"Oh, not much, just now. I get hungry in the night, and my cook knows it. She always leaves me a little snack. But, please, have some more of the rice." She heaped it into his bowl. "Pickles, too. More tea?"

Saiko looked up at me, and then down at the food. She reached out for her bowl, full to the brim with glistening white rice.

Ichiro tore hungrily into another bite of salmon. Okui picked up a bowl of soup and sipped, and smiled.

Never eat first. Let others eat while you watch. Food makes adults into children. They let their guard down. Keep yours up.

Still, I could not help thinking that the soup, at least, must be all right. Okui was drinking it herself. And the servants had brought out a covered tureen and ladled us each a bowl; it was not as if they could have poisoned one drop and left the rest harmless.

I drank salty soup and steaming tea, and watched Ichiro and Saiko for signs of imminent death or drugged drowsiness. They showed none. I reached out slowly for one of the sweet cakes. Years ago, when I was younger than Ichiro, I'd watched Madame eating one. I'd smelled the sweet rice flour. She'd dipped each bite in wine and licked her fingers afterward. She must have known I was staring, though she'd never looked my way.

Cautiously I opened my mouth and took a bite. I'd never tasted anything so soft, or so sweet. It slipped down my throat and seemed to make me hungrier than ever.

I gave in. If we were to be poisoned, we'd all die together.

Okui smiled with what looked like genuine delight as I piled my bowl high, a delicious sensation of well-being sliding along my arms and down my legs with each soft, succulent bite.

When not even Ichiro could shovel in another mouthful, Okui led us into a nearby room. Servants filed in with steaming buckets and left with empty ones. A waist-high wooden tub was soon full of scalding water.

"Your mistress," I said to the girl who had brought in the tea. "Is she . . ."

Going to poison us? Slit our throats while we sleep? Sell news of us to anyone following?

"Do you have enough water, now? Is it nice and hot?" Okui's voice came from behind me. The girl emptied her bucket into the tub and scuttled away without meeting my eyes. I'd have to try more questions later.

Saiko was already stripping off her kimono, and admonishing Ichiro for attempting to climb into the steaming tub before he'd sluiced himself clean with water from the buckets on the floor. "Do you think we want to be soaking with your filthy feet?" she scolded, and Okui laughed.

"No, please!" I said sharply to another serving girl, as she reached out to pull my jacket from my shoulders. She flinched.

"Do let her take it. She can get it clean before morning," Okui said.

"I wouldn't dream of putting anyone to the trouble," I said firmly, keeping my hands on the jacket. I certainly didn't need a servant to find the things I kept in my pockets.

"Oh, it's no bother—well. If you'd really rather. Here, do take Saiko's—isn't that your name, dear?—kimono. Make sure it's clean. And yours, Ichiro, my dear, such a rip there. Here, girl, you can sew that up tonight."

No harm in letting her servants busy themselves with Ichiro and Saiko's clothes, I supposed. But I made sure my own stayed safe, by the simple device of refusing to take them off until everyone but the three of us had left the room.

"Adventures," Ichiro sighed, neck-deep in hot water. "Not as difficult as I thought."

"Kata? Aren't you coming in?" Saiko paused, stepping over the tub's high rim.

My skin felt pebbled with sweat and grime. I had road dust on my face and pine pitch in my hair and my sore knee had started throbbing more painfully than ever, as if urging me to climb into that hot water and soak some of the ache out. But if we were all three of us up to our chins, who'd be on guard?

"After," I said, a little grimly. "And you hurry!"

"Hurry a bath? Why?"

I rolled my eyes. "So you can watch the door while *I* take one." I wasn't about to be the only one of us who was stinking.

The servants brought clean clothes, and Saiko slipped on a white kimono while I eased myself into the tub. "Oh . . . silk," she said softly, to no one.

There was a kimono for Ichiro too, this one soft blue, and another for me. I left it on the floor, and pulled my own gritty, dusty clothes on after I'd climbed out of the lukewarm water, feeling like a snake trying to wriggle back into its discarded skin.

"Here," Saiko said softly, coming up behind me. I

turned quickly to face her, my eyes going to her hand, which held—a comb?

"Don't be silly. Turn back around. It'll be easier if you sit down." She found a bench and pushed me onto it. "Hold still."

"Ouch!"

"I said, hold still." Maybe she didn't know what to do with a sword, but her fingers were deft with a comb. I still kept an eye on the door, but I felt the muscles in my neck and back slowly relaxing under her touch, as she teased and tugged the knots out of my hair. Ichiro watched as he slipped his own kimono on. I made a face at him. He flicked water from a bucket at me and laughed.

When we came back into the main room, Okui was on her knees, rolling out four futons. No thin mats or mattresses padded with crackling straw for her—these were stuffed with cotton, inches thick.

"Why are you doing that yourself, mistress?" Ichiro hurried to help her.

"Oh, my servants have left. Back to their village. They don't stay the night."

I felt a heavy little thud deep in my gut, as if I'd swallowed lead rather than sweet rice cakes. I'd wasted time soaking and letting Saiko fuss over my hair, and I'd missed my chance to question the servants.

"Saiko, that kimono looks lovely on you. Your skin was made for silk. And . . . Kata. Didn't they . . . ?"

"I like my own clothes best," I said shortly.

"Just as you please, of course. There, thank you, Ichiro. Put my mattress in the corner, will you? And here." She was opening a cupboard, pulling out soft quilts. "Such a young gentleman. Handsome as well!" Ichiro blushed as he hurried to make the beds. "Did you have enough to eat? Are you still hungry at all?" Near her own futon was a low table, and on it were trays with bowls and plates and a small teapot with a deep brown glaze. "If you want a little snack in the nighttime . . . Of course, Ichiro, a cake before bed. Here, take this one; it looks delicious."

I came up behind Saiko as she was pulling her damp hair into a braid. "We can't all sleep at once," I said quietly in her ear.

I expected her to argue, to tell me I was foolishly anxious, but her fingers paused in her hair for a moment before she nodded. She understood.

Okui was generous. Hospitable. Kind.

Much too kind.

No one took in strangers like this, these days. No one had storerooms of expensive food to share. No one lived without a hint of fear.

I'd dropped my guard, seduced by a bath and a feast, and missed an opportunity to gather intelligence. It had been a serious mistake. Worse than that. It had been weakness. And I could not repair it now. All I could do was keep on the alert. I'd have Saiko to help.

She took the first watch while I stretched myself out on a mattress as soft as a cloud, cushioning every muscle, easing every ache. Saiko silently nudged me awake when the moon was high, sending light between the shutters to lie in pale lines across the floor.

I glanced at Ichiro, flat on his back and snoring lightly.

177

When I looked up, I found myself meeting Saiko's gaze. Quick as thought, we shared an indulgent look—*oh, let him rest.*

Then she lay down, pulling a quilt over herself, and I sat upright on my own futon, letting the time pass.

The trick to staying alert on watch is not to think. Thinking slows time. You let your mind go blank, and sounds float into that blankness, like fish swimming one by one through a fathomless pool.

Ichiro's snores. Saiko's breathing settling, slowing, deepening.

A cricket rasping outside, like a file against metal. An owl calling like a lost and hungry ghost.

The cloth of my jacket rubbing against my skin as I shifted my weight.

A rustle from the futon in the corner.

As quickly as I could, I lay down, curled on my side, tucking a hand under my right cheek. Whatever Okui was about to do, she must not find me watching.

She sat up, silently. A simple kimono, this one plain, undyed cotton, was wrapped around her body. Her hair, loose, reached to the floor, and swayed with each movement.

I could see her face clearly in a stripe of moonlight. Her eyes were closed. Was she sleepwalking?

Without glancing at any of the quiet bodies on the floor, she slid gracefully off her futon to kneel by the table with the food, and turned her head so that the moonlight caught her profile again. Her eyes had not opened.

I felt my heartbeat quicken a little. It was more than her

own movements that were stirring her hair now.

I'd heard of a creature called an octopus, a many-legged monster from under the sea. Now I felt I was watching one. Tendrils of Okui's hair lifted and stretched, reaching out. They hesitated, then dove down. One delicately removed a lid from a red lacquered bowl. Another picked up a sweet rice cake.

The strands of hair on the back of Okui's head parted to reveal a second mouth there, the lips curling back hungrily. Our kind and generous hostess was as much a demon as the centipede who had tried to rip open my throat in the school kitchen.

Did her servants know? I wondered, fascinated, as the tentacles of hair lifted one bite after another into the waiting mouth. One strand even poured a cup of tea, and another lifted it toward those eager lips. Was that why those villagers fled the house at night? And what about the rich man who visited here? Did *he* know what slept beside him in bed?

Okui's eyelids never fluttered as the mouth on the back of her head chewed and swallowed and slurped. A new thought struck me, and it seemed more horrible than any of the others.

Did *she* know? Okui herself? Could you be a demon and never know it?

Okui lifted her head quickly, as if she'd heard something. But I knew I hadn't made a sound.

I didn't forget to breathe slowly and deeply, as if I were sleeping. And I knew she could not see my face, even if her eyes had been open. I'd deliberately chosen to lay my futon in a pitch-black corner, away from windows.

Her hair laid a bowl of rice neatly on the table, and she rose. As she made her way across the room, with her peaceful and sleeping face turned toward me, that hair coiled and writhed around her head, each tendril seeming to sniff at the air.

If I woke Okui from her sleep now, what would happen? Would she be horrified, even driven mad, to discover what she was? Or would I simply be facing a conscious enemy, rather than one who was half asleep?

What I needed here was an ally. How could I rouse Saiko or Ichiro without shaking Okui from her walking dream?

Okui's toes were inches from my futon. She turned her back toward me, and something slipped from her hair. A chopstick. It clattered lightly against the floor.

Stealthily, I reached for the chopstick, grabbed it, and flicked it hard at Saiko. I heard it hit something soft—had it been her futon or her flesh?

The curving ropes of Okui's hair seemed to hesitate. They were blind; they could not see my movements. But could they somehow sense what I was doing? Had my arm made waves and ripples in the air that her hair could feel?

Still facing away from me, Okui knelt gracefully beside my futon. Curious, searching, the long strands of hair reached for me.

Two brushed my face, feather-light. One lifted open the front of my jacket and another reached inside toward the secret pocket there, fondling the pearl through the cloth like a blind beggar stroking a cherished coin.

A fifth tendril slipped slowly around my neck.

I heard the faintest gasp from Saiko. She was awake. Good.

I sat up abruptly, and my right hand, holding my knife, came out from under my cheek to slash through the rope of hair twined about my neck.

Okui screamed, the sound doubled as it came from two throats. I punched her as hard as I could in the mouth on the back of her head, sending her sprawling, facedown, to the floor.

Moments stretched out as they do sometimes in battle, as if I had minutes to consider every move.

Saiko leapt from her bed to fling open the screen and unlatch the shutters of the nearest window. Moonlight streamed in.

Ichiro sat up, kicking off his quilt, looking baffled.

Okui, on the floor, whirled to face me. Now her eyes were open. Crouched like an animal, she bared her teeth, and her hair reared up over her head, a dozen snakes poised to strike.

"Out!" I shouted.

Ichiro had the good sense to snatch up his sandals before diving through the open window.

I sprang off my bed, grabbed my quilt, and threw it at Okui. It hit her right in the face, and her hair seized hold of the slippery silk, wrestling with it, blinding her further.

Saiko was out the window now. I grabbed my pack and followed, or tried to.

Before I made it outside, something soft but heavy as a cudgel slammed into the backs of my knees, knocking me down. My forehead cracked hard against the window frame, and everything around me went black, and sticky, and slow.

My senses came back in a moment, but that moment was too long. A black rope had already seized my shoulders and flipped me over onto my back, and Okui loomed above me, her face one ravenous snarl.

There was a heavy weight on my legs, so I could not kick. A snake of hair lashed at my eyes. I threw up my right arm to fend it off and now my wrist was pinioned, the knife in that hand useless. White froth bubbled at the corners of Okui's mouth.

Then something heavy smashed through the window and smacked Okui full in the face.

She shrieked like a wounded bird. The hair around my wrist loosened.

The tree branch, for that's what it was, swung back and hit Okui again. I wrenched my arm free, slashed with my knife, and caught her cheek. She howled, falling back, and I wondered how she'd explain a knife wound to the man who owned her, the next time he came to visit.

The weight on my legs was gone. Hands seized me and hauled me out through the window. Saiko and I fell to the ground in a heap, and Ichiro slammed his branch at the window again, giving us time to scramble out of reach.

I looked back to see Okui gripping the window frame, her hair storming about her bloodstained face. But she made no move to climb out after us.

"You'll wish you'd stayed inside with me," she spat. It was awful to see what rage and thwarted hunger did to her face. And before I could react, her hair seized the shutter and slammed it shut.

SIXTEEN

The path we'd followed to reach Okui's house had vanished. To my right, the white stones in the grass still glimmered in the moonlight, but now they led from the plum tree with its ghosts of blossoms straight to a dense thicket of vines and thorns.

"What *was* she?" Ichiro gasped.

We retreated to the left across the clearing, moving away from the house. Here no thicket blocked our way, and we pushed between cedars and young oak trees, stumbling over roots, clutching at each other for balance.

"Another bakemono. A double-mouthed woman," Saiko answered, her voice low. "You've heard of them."

"Hearing isn't seeing." Ichiro's voice sounded unsteady, as if he were shivering. "Kata? Are you all right?"

I nodded before I remembered that they couldn't see me. "All right," I whispered. Then I spat out a curse.

My pack. My pack!

It had slipped from my hand when my head had struck the windowsill. My sword had been in there. A tinderbox for lighting fires. Most of our money, too, although I'd tucked a few coins into various pockets for safekeeping. What a fool I was, my brains addled by one good thump. How would we manage now?

"What's wrong?" Ichiro was worried. "Did she hurt you?"

I breathed in slowly, breathed out even more slowly. The pack was gone. There was no getting it back. It would do no good to worry Ichiro over the loss, or to curse myself.

In the darkness, I found Ichiro's arm and patted it clumsily. "No. I'm not hurt." I'd have a lump on my forehead, but that was all. The demon had not injured me badly, though she'd been close enough.

That mouth, with the lips pulling back from the teeth, like a snarling cat's. Had she wanted the pearl, or had she been hungry? Or both?

It didn't much matter. The only reason I had not been a meal for a demon was the tree branch in Ichiro's hands and Saiko's quick thinking.

Trust no friend farther than you can see her. Trust no ally for more than you've paid him.

They could have run. The two of them had been well outside the window, and Okui's attention had been on me.

But they'd stayed. They'd fought. For me.

"Which way?" Saiko murmured. "Should we wait until light?"

It was a good question. I'd been disoriented by the time we'd reached Okui's door. Now—hopeless. Even for a gold coin, I could not have told you which way was north.

But I was fairly sure we should not wait for the sun to rise.

There was something under my feet, and I was feeling distinctly uneasy about it. I moved a step, felt something roll, and then heard it crunch.

I knelt, forcing back my distaste, and felt among dry leaves and brittle twigs.

A jacket and trousers of soft cotton. Something long as a stout branch, but smoother. Something delicate, tapering and curved. Something round as a melon, and about that size.

A lucky gleam of moonlight struck through the branches overhead and confirmed what I had already guessed.

Bones. I'd been standing on bones.

The clothing was a mottled brown, good for hiding among trees and brush. And before the clouds whisked the light away, I spotted two long slim bones side by side. A long, narrow strip of cloth had been wrapped many times around the bones where their ends had fused together, and a nest of small white finger bones spilled from the bandage.

It was the kind of field dressing someone might tie around a broken wrist.

Instructor Willow was not tracking us anymore. She must have avoided the bandits, gotten ahead of us through the pass, and guessed correctly that once we had done the same we would head for the only shelter in sight.

Had Willow entered Okui's house as well? Did the double-mouthed woman toss the bones of her meals into the forest for crows and foxes and beetles to gnaw? Or had the instructor stayed outside, watching for us under the trees, and met something here she was not trained to fight? Something that could suck all the flesh from a body while leaving the clothes—and even a bandage—untouched?

Okui had said we would wish we'd stayed inside with her. As if there were something beneath the moon worse than being trapped in the house of a hungry demon.

"Downhill," I said grimly, answering Saiko, as I got to my feet.

I should never have let us go into that house. I should have known from the beginning that something was wrong. Good food, soft beds, hot baths—was it that easy to throw me off my guard? What kind of a ninja was I?

And now I was lost.

It was worse than stumbling through the gardens in the castle of Ichiro's uncle. Then it had been wood and water and stone against me. Here I felt as if the night itself was fighting back, clawing at our skin with thorny hands, clinging to our hair with dark tendrils, slithering underfoot to make us trip and stumble.

Darkness was supposed to be my ally. Did the night know how badly I'd failed? Was this my punishment?

I untied my wide cloth belt and gripped the loop on one end with my left hand. I gave the other end of the belt to Saiko. Ichiro held on between. We straggled down the slope, ducking under branches we could only dimly see, stumbling over roots, slipping on drifts of pine needles. When one fell, the other two did as well. But at least we stayed together. Maybe I wasn't the ninja I'd once thought myself, but whatever my failures, I'd gotten the three of us this far. I wasn't about to let the predatory darkness swallow any of us up.

We'd paused for a breath when I heard it. A heavy, soft footfall. I heard it again, when we started moving once more.

My eyes were useless. It was a world of gray and black, every shadow darker than ink. Anything could stay hidden just by standing still.

All I had were my ears, and I wasn't sure what they were telling me.

The footsteps were too quiet to be booted feet, too heavy to be a fox or a badger, too stealthy for a bear. I'd heard of a giant cat with fur like a flaming coal. The thought made me want to dash for a mouse hole. Even climbing a tree would not save us from a hungry, hunting cat.

Then claws skittered on rock. Cats don't hunt with their claws out.

"Did you hear . . ." Saiko whispered.

"What?" Ichiro sounded panicked.

"Nothing!" I said sharply. "Keep going!"

There was no point in whispering. The thing knew we were there.

A faint, dull glimmer up ahead hinted at an end to the dense forest. Would whatever was tracking us stay in the trees? Or would it spring when it sensed we might escape?

Full-grown trees were giving way to saplings and scrubby bushes. Slower walking. I went first, breaking a path as best I could.

Something scuttled through the tall grass to my left. Something whipped through the air, too quickly for me to spot.

Something sighed, a vast exhalation of breath.

"Just the wind," Saiko said firmly, before Ichiro could ask.

"This way." I pushed forward. It was better to be a moving target than a standing one.

We broke out from under the trees. Moonlight burst down as we kicked loose from brush and vines, shadows clinging to us like cobwebs. I thought we'd done it. We were free. We could run.

Actually, we could fall.

My eyes, dazzled by moonlight, didn't see that the ground gave way right where the forest ended. There was a steep earthen bank. I rolled down it. Since Saiko and Ichiro were still holding the belt, they both fell with me. We all ended up on hands and knees in thick, greedy mud.

We struggled to our feet, and I tried to get my bearings. We'd landed on a river plain, the one we'd seen from the ridge earlier. That meant that somewhere not too far from here was the road.

A road was good. It meant firm ground for running, and clear lines of sight in at least two directions. It meant people. A road was made by humans, and would lead to humans. I hoped.

A glint of light in the distance might be the river. The road had run alongside of it. So for now, that river was our destination.

"I'm sinking!" Saiko wailed. I groaned, splashed to her side, seized her arm, and dragged her over to a clump of stringy grass. One end of my belt was still in my hand. I thrust the other end at her.

"Hold this and follow me," I told her. "Walk where the grass grows. That way you won't—Ichiro! Stay over here!"

"Come this way!" the boy called back. He was already farther away than I liked.

"You don't know how to do this!" I growled, and stepped into the muck, pulling Saiko after me. "Wait!"

And then I heard it. Or rather, I didn't.

Everything became still. All the forest sounds that had become so familiar vanished.

Whatever had been tracking us had slunk to the earthen bank above our heads. It wanted to reach us before we'd gotten far.

"Run!" I yelled, so that Ichiro could hear, too. "But— Ichiro, no! Watch where you're going!"

Ahead of us, Ichiro sprang over pools and puddles, his feet seeming to find a secure clump of earth each time. But his luck wouldn't last; it couldn't.

What madness was this? Why was I following *him*? He was nothing but a child. He wasn't trained. He was no shadow warrior, no warrior at all. He'd be up to his chin any minute now, and then what would I do? Keep running and leave him? Stay to haul him out and be eaten?

I dragged Saiko forward, stumbling and slipping. "Ichiro, *wait!*" I shouted, slid off a clump of soggy moss, and fell in myself.

I was up to my knees. The mud was sharply cold, and it seized my feet and calves tight. I let go of my belt as I went down, so I would not pull Saiko in with me. Even so, she staggered and fell to her hands and knees, luckily landing safe in a patch of grass.

But she dropped the belt, and it flopped into a patch of muddy water, too far for either of us to reach.

Nausea, as cold as the mud that held me, surged up in my gut. A ninja shouldn't fear death. I'd thought I didn't. But to be trapped here—stuck, helpless—waiting for claws to rip me, teeth to tear my muscles from my bones—

Darkness was closing in. Clouds sliding over the moon? No, a thick bank of fog had rolled over us.

No sign of Ichiro. The idiot boy was probably drowning somewhere. I tried to work my left leg free, and then my right. I wasn't sinking. I could get out of this. But not quickly. It would take time. I didn't *have* time.

"Give me your jacket," Saiko called. "I can pull you out with it. Hurry!"

My hand had gone to my collar when a long snake flew out of the darkness and slapped me in the face.

"Grab it!" Ichiro's voice.

It wasn't a snake at all; it was a thick, soft vine. I seized it. "Now!" the boy called. He'd braced himself. I clutched the vine and pulled. It held. Ichiro's weight gave it strength, and I dragged myself free.

"Follow the vine!"

This fog—where had it come from? It stung my eyes and was bitter in my throat. Blind, I let the vine lead me. Ahead of me, Saiko had grasped it, too.

We both crawled, splashing through mud and water, but somehow Ichiro had found a safe path. We didn't sink. Then the earth sloped up under our hands and feet. We were on a dirt causeway that cut across the swamp.

How had Ichiro known this was here?

The nausea hadn't left me. Now it doubled. I put my head down and crawled forward on the raised dirt roadway, too dizzy to try to stand. I'd felt this bad only once before, when I'd been a child, back at the school. I'd lain on my mat with a fever for three days. Even Madame had come to look at me, and a priest had brought medicines, bitter to swallow, that only made me feel sicker than ever.

It had been Masako who'd crept away from the practice yard every chance she got to wipe my face with wet cloths and whisper encouragement in my ear. *You will get better, Kata. This will pass, Kata. Soon.* Twice she'd brought me soup from her own bowl and spooned it, a trickle at a time, into my mouth.

And oddly enough, now Masako was next to me. Her plain face had grown pretty, though, and she was wearing an elegant kimono of white silk and ornaments as white as bone in her hair.

How funny that she should be here, in this swamp at night. But I was glad to see her. I didn't think I'd ever thanked her for taking care of me, so long ago. Now I'd have a chance.

"Close your eyes!" she ordered me.

A funny thing to ask anyone to do. It was not as if I were going to bed. But now the thought of sleep was in my head, and I could not get it out. How long since I'd lain down in a bed and gotten to stay there? How long since I'd rested without being up half the night on watch, or being attacked by hungry demons, or kidnapped by courteous bandits? Sleep, yes. I would go to sleep. I'd feel so much better when I woke up.

Masako actually growled at me, and she seized my arm and gave me a shake. "Close your eyes!" she insisted.

Before I could do it, Ichiro screamed.

Some of the black fog seemed to have blown away. I could see Saiko now, on her knees, both hands to her head. Ichiro crouched behind her, and his back was to me. He was staring at something crawling up the causeway.

Masako was shouting something. Something strange. It seemed to be, "Don't look!"

But of course I had to look. How else could I know what I was fighting? I was fighting something, wasn't I? I always was.

I saw—

It was only for a heartbeat, before I turned away. But in that moment, I saw a roiling black shadow that reminded me a bit of Okui's hair: alive, furious, ravenous.

Inside the dark mass was a snake's tail, lashing madly. Flaming stripes blazed along the thing's back. There seemed to be a small, furry head, and in it a monkey's mouth screeched, with a sound that drove into my ears like a nail. It hurt to look at the crawling thing. Pain jabbed into my

193

eyes, blossomed and burst in my head.

My stomach heaved, and before I knew it, I was throwing up into the dirt. My eyes closed tightly as the spasm squeezed my stomach and throat, but in that instant, my mind cleared a bit, and I knew what was attacking us.

I groped, seized Saiko's arm, and shook her. "Shut your eyes!" I ordered, without opening mine. "Ichiro! You, too! Shut your eyes!"

A nue. Merely to be near it could bring on the wrenching illness that had seized us all. Trying to look at it would only make things worse. My single glance had made me feel like my brain had been tied into knots inside my skull.

I pushed myself to my knees, and then unsteadily to my feet.

"Down!" I shouted. "Flat!"

I hoped their minds were clear enough to obey me.

I'd sparred while blindfolded often enough. I'd made my way from the school's storeroom to the roof, and from there to the ground, without using my sight. But during those times, I'd been able to count on my brain and my sense of balance. I hadn't been trapped in a black whirlwind inside my own head.

Clumsily I slid one of my knives out of its sheath at my wrist. Stroked the smooth, chilly steel with my fingertips. Pricked the pad of my left thumb with the point.

Sharp, clear pain. It steadied my brain and gave me something to focus on. Now I was able to bring my attention to my ears.

Dizzy, disoriented, I had little idea where I was, and more importantly, where the others were. Saiko was beside me; I could feel her huddled at my feet. But Ichiro? Masako? Where were they?

And what *was* Masako doing here, out in the middle of a swamp at night?

Think about that later. Now, listen. *Listen.*

A frightened moan. Saiko. Panicked breathing. Ichiro. A long, eager hiss. A ravenous snarl.

There.

I gripped the knife by its black blade and sent it winging straight at that growl, praying it would not hit any of my friends along the way.

A yelp, a whine, like an injured dog. Had the knife hit the fox?

Because of course the woman in the white kimono had been the fox spirit, not Masako. My mind was clearing by the second, and I knew the truth. Masako was back at the school. Not out here in the middle of a haunted swamp. Not with me.

I risked a glance and sank down to my knees, covering my eyes with my hands, as the sight of the thing writhing on the path twisted my senses into merciless tangles. Small, so much smaller than I'd thought. The nue was not any larger than my fox. And clearly my knife had hit its target.

Something rolled and splashed into the mud and floundered off loudly through the swamp. The nausea eased. I took a slow breath and cautiously lowered my hands.

Saiko looked shaken, but she stood. Ichiro grabbed my hand, let me pull him up, and then stumbled a few steps to throw up in the mud.

I looked around for my knife, but it was nowhere to be

seen. The nue was gone, and it must have taken my weapon with it. That meant it was wounded, but alive.

Something barked once, sharply. An order. I looked up and glimpsed a white shape on the causeway ahead of me.

"That way," Ichiro said, wiping his mouth and pointing. "We should follow it."

"Wait."

Brother and sister looked up at me, surprised.

"It showed me the way through the swamp," Ichiro explained. "Kata, it's here to help us. Look where it wants us to go!"

The causeway led to a bridge. The bridge led to a road. The road wound uphill. Even in the darkness, I could see what was on the crown of that hill—a curving wall, a massive gate, a tall tower with a tiered roof beyond.

A temple, the one I'd glimpsed from the ridge before nightfall. Surely the demons of the forest and swamp would not follow us there. Surely we'd be safe.

Unless that was exactly what the fox wanted us to think.

She had just helped us face a nue. She'd saved us in the warlord's garden. She'd kept watch over us by the river and in the mountains—although she'd stayed away from Okui's house. There she'd been wiser than I had been.

She also knew about the pearl. She wanted it for herself. Had all her help been meant to make us believe her just when we should not?

Trust no friend. Trust no ally.

Would the fox lead us to safety? Or a trap?

"Kata, she saved us. I think she's a spirit. A good one." Ichiro took a few steps along the causeway, then looked back

196

at his sister and at me. "Please. I'm sure it's all right. Please. Trust me."

I started forward, and Saiko followed. The fox turned and darted ahead of Ichiro, running along the causeway, soon disappearing into the night.

"You think he's right?" Saiko murmured at my back. "You trust a fox?"

"No," I said grimly. "That's not why."

I was thinking of the nue I had injured. I'd always heard that nue were giant creatures, as big as houses. Perhaps it wasn't true. Perhaps they only made themselves seem so. If no one could get a good look at one, how could anyone know for sure?

The creature my knife had struck might have been the normal size for a nue. Or it might have been . . .

Saiko gasped when I told her, in a voice too low for Ichiro to hear, what I was thinking.

"It might have been young," she whispered.

Young creatures often had mothers nearby. The thought was enough to push our feet a little faster, to catch up with Ichiro, to hurry toward the river, and the bridge, and the temple.

Just a little farther to run.

SEVENTEEN

We avoided the main gate, of course. It was magnificently carved and gilded and unlikely to open for anyone less than a saint. But no temple or castle has only one gate. We worked our way around the wall until we found a small back entrance for servants, deliveries, and humble travelers looking for shelter.

This gate did have a gatekeeper, and he was in no hurry to open up.

I could hardly blame him. His job was to keep suspicious characters out, and while we didn't seem very threatening, we did look, at least, a bit odd.

Saiko was in the silk kimono that Okui had given her, although what was left of it was no longer white. Ichiro's kimono was no better, and though I had my own clothes on, I'd lost a sandal in the swamp and had a swollen bruise on my forehead from Okui's windowsill. We were all scratched and battered and wearing more mud than anything else.

But I made sure to have Saiko ask for admittance. And when tears welled up in her perfect eyes, the man gave in. Most men would.

She blotted her cheeks delicately dry on a nearly-clean spot of her sleeve and gave the gatekeeper a grateful bow after he'd unbarred the gate, and I swear he would have taken off her sandals for her and brought her tea.

I gave her a sidelong look as we hurried in, and one corner of her mouth quirked in a very brief smile.

"Visitors? So late?" a mild voice asked.

I was tired. The night had been long, and uncomfortable, and more than reasonably terrifying. But that was no excuse. It had been years since anyone had gotten within ten paces of me without being noticed. Now this man, the one who'd asked the question, was standing just a little behind the gatekeeper, and I couldn't say how he had arrived.

Granted, this particular person seemed harmless—an old monk, no taller than I was, in a yellow-orange robe a little too big for him, a strand of simple wooden prayer beads twisted about one wrist. His head was shaved and his smile was gentle. Not a threat. But that was no excuse. I should have seen him, and I hadn't.

Worse, I thought, he'd seen *me*.

When he'd spoken, I'd jumped. And my hand had twitched toward my last remaining knife. The monk's gaze had flicked my way, so quickly it would have been easy to miss.

I hadn't noticed him, and he had noticed me. That wasn't what was supposed to happen.

The gatekeeper was stumbling over his own tongue. "Just children, Tosabo. Alone. Out in the night. Could I have left them out there? Bandits and ghosts and foxes, you know."

"Bandits and ghosts would be a nice relief, actually," Ichiro muttered under his breath. I gave my head a quick shake, to hush him.

"He was very kind," Saiko said, glancing up gratefully at the gatekeeper before casting her eyes demurely down. "We were so frightened . . ." The kimono sleeve again blotted at her eyes.

And the monk was . . . unimpressed. His face stayed expressionless. Saiko usually prompted a response of some sort from men, monks or not. But this one was different.

"You're safe now, little one," the gatekeeper soothed. "I've a daughter of my own at home. Wouldn't like to see her out on such a night. I was just going to inform the abbot, of course. Right away. Of course."

"Oh, we'll let the abbot have his rest," the monk, Tosabo, said pleasantly. "I can take charge of them."

And so he did, leading us to a small, windowless guest room. I would have preferred a room that had more than one way to leave it, but I had neither an excuse nor the energy to object. With his own hands Tosabo brought us tea and rice and pickled vegetables, water to wash in, bedding, an oil lamp. He listened patiently to our story of the cruel parents who had cast us out and the aunt we were trying to reach and the path we had lost in the darkness, and finally he bowed before leaving us for the night. Warm. Fed and comfortable. Sheltered by stone walls, prayers, and mantras, surely as safe from demons as we could possibly be.

So why did I feel that there was a threat somewhere here? Or perhaps not a threat, exactly. Something else, undefined. Something that was not quite as it should be.

Was it merely that, at last, I had to admit to myself what had truly happened to Raku?

It was a simple enough deduction. She must be as dead as Instructor Willow. If she wasn't, she would never have allowed us to get this far.

I could tell my heart that I had not done it, that the lonely ghost had destroyed Raku just as the nue—or perhaps its mother?—had probably eaten Willow. But of course, Raku would not have stood at the edge of that rushing river if I had not held my blade at her throat.

I'd been trained all my life to kill. I should have been able to take a life as easily as I picked a lock. But I didn't seem able to do so. And I had never thought my first kill would be . . . one of us. Another deadly flower.

I'd faced Raku in the practice yard. I'd knelt beside her at meals. I'd fallen asleep to the sound of her breathing.

She would not have blamed me or sought revenge. She had understood. Our missions had collided; that was all. And neither of us could go forward until one of us was dead.

Maybe it was these thoughts that made me neglect a warrior's first duty and stare into the dark long after Saiko and Ichiro were asleep.

Or maybe it was simply that Tosabo had not believed a word we'd said.

I'd thought so, as we'd told our story, and I had to admit I'd been impressed. It was not every man—monk or not—who could catch a lie coming from Saiko's lips. And Tosabo proved me right, the next morning, when he followed the servant who brought in tea and millet porridge and knelt to light the lamp. With no windows, the room was dark even though enough hours had passed to bring the dawn.

"So," Tosabo said, as he knelt down beside us and took a cup of tea. The servant bowed and left the room, sliding the screen shut behind him. The monk rolled the small cup between his palms but did not sip. "Morning light may bring truth with it. Tell me again, before I go to see the abbot, what you were doing outside our gate in the middle of the night."

"Holy one," Saiko began, all innocence. "We are trying to reach our family, as I told you, and we lost our way—"

"My dear." He set down his cup and held up his hand to stop her. "You lie very prettily, but that will not get us any farther along our path. It seems that all three of you need some help. I cannot provide it if I do not know the truth."

"Our aunt—" Saiko began again, but I shook my head.

"Safety for the night is all the help we needed to ask," I said, and got to my feet. "Now it's light, and we'll be going."

"Not if I don't tell them to unlock that door." Tosabo smiled brightly at me. "Kneel down, my dear. More tea? Let's talk."

Here it was, the trap I'd sensed last night, sprung while

I'd been slurping porridge. But why was this monk, Tosabo, inside the trap with us?

"Yes, yes, my dear, I've no doubt you're armed," he said peacefully, still smiling, after I'd put my fist through the door's paper screen—only to discover, painfully, the solid wood panel that had been shut and barred behind it. "I saw that last night. And I've no doubt you think you can make them open that door with a knife to my throat, and probably you could. But I told the servant to be about his duties, and it will be quite a while before anyone else comes along this corridor. You are our only guests at the moment. Travel has become so dangerous lately. So I don't think they'll hear you shouting threats for some time. Meanwhile, we may as well chat. Perhaps you'd like to start by telling me what was chasing you last night?"

I had not knelt again; instead, I was standing over Tosabo, seething. Had I learned nothing from last night? How had I let us walk into two traps in a row? I was furious at myself for being such easy prey. And at the monk, too, for smiling up at me so pleasantly, for sitting there so calmly, for knowing all he seemed to know.

"There was . . . something in the swamp," I said guardedly. "It chased us. Something . . . not natural. We didn't say because we thought no one would believe us."

"I am quite skilled at belief. Do please continue."

"There's not much more to tell." I shrugged and knelt down, warily. "We didn't see what it was—"

"Yes, we—"

"Exactly." I talked over Ichiro, raising my voice a little.

"We were frightened, and we ran, and got lost. Then we saw the temple. We knew we'd be safe here."

Tosabo nodded, and said nothing.

Neither did I.

Tosabo seemed perfectly content to sit there. He didn't even seem to be waiting for anything. He was just sitting.

Ichiro fidgeted, opened his mouth, looked up at me, and closed it.

I could wait, too. I'd answered the monk's question. It was his turn.

Saiko touched an eyebrow. Smoothed her hair. Twice. A third time.

But I usually had something to *do* while I waited. A plan to carry out. Knots to untie. An enemy to observe. A wall to scale. A river to swim.

Here, I had nothing. Nothing but a bare room with a locked door and the sound of four people breathing.

Saiko's breath was quiet but a little quick. Ichiro's was nervous, uneven. Mine, impatient. Tosabo's steady, calm, almost inaudible.

"A nue," Ichiro burst out. "It was a nue!"

"Ichiro!" Saiko and I both snapped together, sounding equally like older sisters. The boy needed to keep his mouth shut. Once he started talking about demons, what else might he be led to reveal?

"We have to. Kata, Saiko, we have to. Listen. He could help us! He might know . . . things." Ichiro shifted his attention from us to the monk. "It was a nue, and it was after us."

My hand itched to slap the boy. But what good would it do now? He'd already fallen into the old monk's trap, baited so expertly with silence. At least he had not been fool enough to mention *why* the demon had been on our trail.

"Really, it was after Kata," Ichiro explained. "She has a jewel. A pearl. It was in our family, but now it's hers. And the demons want it."

Or, then again, he had.

Ichiro had been seized by some madness of trust, and he poured everything out to Tosabo—the pearl, his family, his father's death, the plot against his life, our harried trek toward his uncle and possible safety there. Ghosts and demons, bakemono, stories whispered in the dark come gruesomely to life.

"And the nue in the swamp, it was *awful*. But Kata threw her knife at it, didn't you, Kata? And then, well, then we ran here." A little breathless, Ichiro finished his speech at last.

"We saw the temple," I said again. Certainly I was not going to add to Ichiro's indiscretions by bringing up the fox spirit that had been trailing us. Helping us. Or possibly stalking us. Which?

"I see." Tosabo nodded, and his eyes moved thoughtfully from one of us to the other—Ichiro eager and full of words, Saiko with eyes meekly downcast—you had to know her well to catch the tightness at the corner of her mouth and in her shoulders that said she was angry, or anxious, or both. And last, at me.

"I knew—well, the entire countryside knows—that there is a search underway for the Kashihara heir," Tosabo said thoughtfully. "And he has been with the two of you all this time, safe and secret. Remarkable. Even more so, now that I know exactly what has been hunting all of you. May I see it? This pearl?"

I would have preferred to keep the jewel hidden . . . but what harm could it do to let this monk see it? He already knew it existed. Slowly I reached inside my jacket. Carefully I took out the pearl and let it lie on my palm.

Where did it get that unearthly glow, in this dim room lit only by the small flame of the lamp? The gold ring around the jewel looked almost dark against that other-worldly light.

Tosabo bent forward and I drew my hand back.

"Have no fear, child. I do want not to take it from you. Indeed, I would much prefer not to touch it at all. I've heard of such things, but to *see* one . . . My old eyes have trouble believing it; that is all." He sat back, shaking his head. "Do you know, exactly, what you are holding there? No, I can see you do not. And you two?" Tosabo's attention swooped like a hawk toward Ichiro and Saiko. "This thing has been in your family, you say? For generations? Do *you* know what it is? Three children carrying *that* around the countryside!"

Saiko leaned forward, her eyes, for once, off her knees. "No one told us," she said.

"My father would have told me," Ichiro said, "when I was grown. But he . . . he . . ."

"Died. Bloodily, I've no doubt. Oh, my dear, I'm sorry, I am. But a bloody death is likely to be the fate of anyone who carries a thing like that about with him."

"A thing like *what*?" I demanded, my words coming out just a few beats before Saiko's.

"My dear, in your hand you hold the soul of a demon."

※　※　※

In a few minutes we were in another room, this one not a windowless cell with a barred door. Tosabo had taken us straight to the abbot, shooing out several servants and a few monks who looked disgruntled at being dismissed like maids so that three children could speak to the leader of the monastery.

The abbot was even older than Tosabo, with a wrinkled face and a bald head as smooth as the pearl. He knelt at a low desk by a window, waiting patiently and silently as Tosabo ordered his monks about. Beside him was the room's only decoration, a screen that reached from floor to ceiling. On it was a painting of a mountain so realistic it looked as if you could step on a rock and start climbing. At the top, clinging to a weathered outcrop, a single ancient cedar had been twisted into knots by the wind.

"Show him," Tosabo told me once we were alone with his abbot. "Oh no, my dear, there's no time for that, truly. We are two old men, and you could kill us both easily, could you not, if you needed to? Save us time and let that mistrust of yours rest. It's served you well, I've no doubt, poor child, but set it aside just for the moment. Show him."

The old man drew in his breath at the sight of the jewel and turned to Tosabo. "You brought this here?"

It was not anger, not yet, but the abbot's voice held the potential for it. Such a wizened little man; his bones looked as fragile as a bird's. But in a way I could not account for, he made me think of Madame.

Tosabo did not flinch. "Any blame falls on me, holy one," he said cheerfully. "But I did not know this was what they carried."

"You did not know," the abbot grumbled. "If there were a silk cord that tied earth to heaven, you would pull it apart and say you did not know."

"My sins are heavy," Tosabo agreed. "But the question is, how many are left?"

Both peered at the pearl in my palm as if it were likely to move.

"How many *what*?" I demanded.

The two old men glanced up at me in surprise, as if they had forgotten I was anything other than a hand.

"See how thin the gold band is?" Tosabo murmured. He'd forgotten me again. "Three, perhaps?"

"Four at the most."

"Three *what*?" I closed my fingers tightly over the pearl and glared.

"Wishes," Tosabo said, shaking his head a little sadly. "Put it away, my dear, do. Dreadful thing. Some foolish sorcerer bound a demon in that pearl, who knows how many years ago. The demon is the servant of the jewel's owner. Like all servants, it must obey."

"And like all prisoners, it longs for freedom," murmured the abbot.

"A certain number of tasks, and the demon is done. Its term of service is over," Tosabo added. "And it will take a price for its service." His eyes were worried. "The soul of the last person to command it."

"So she could . . ." Saiko breathed. She was at my elbow. "Ask for—what? What could it give her?"

"It depends on which demon is inside." The abbot's mouth looked as if he'd bitten into a sour plum. "Some of these demons can grant—well. No matter. Child, do not think of it."

Absurd. How could I not think of it? What could the pearl do for me, if I asked?

What had it *already* done for me?

For one heartbeat I was back up in a tree, staring down at a soldier's helmeted head, wishing desperately that he would move. He had. Then I was lying in the grass, listening to three mounted horsemen gallop up a hill, wishing they would not hear a muffled sneeze. They had not.

Had I spent two wishes on things as simple as that? But I had not known, then. I'd had no idea what kind of a gift Ichiro had given me.

Could the pearl turn me invisible? Teach me to fly? Could I leap over castle walls, transform into mist or smoke, slide through keyholes or under locked doors?

I remembered that dizzying moment of freedom I'd felt in the castle of Ichiro's uncle, Hikosane. That knowledge that I could do anything—*anything*.

And that was when I'd had nothing but myself and my wits and my training to rely on. Now I had so much more.

And I had been planning to *sell* the pearl. For gold. Gold!

"No, my dear." Tosabo was frowning at me. "Do *not* be tempted. What did you plan to do with it?"

"Take it to our uncle," Ichiro explained. "We thought he could—um. Do something. There are rituals, prayers. That kind of thing, to keep the demons away. Maybe you . . . ?"

The abbot shook his bald head. "Even if we did know the proper rituals, I would not let that thing stay here. There are, no doubt, priests who serve your family. They would know exactly what must be done."

I quickly stowed the pearl away inside my jacket once more, tying the pocket tightly shut. I felt Tosabo's sharp eyes on me as I did so.

"Keep it hidden," the abbot said with a nod. "Keep it safe. Most importantly, keep it out of my monastery. Tosabo." He looked sternly at his monk. "Make arrangements, please."

Earlier, Tosabo had asked me if I knew what I held in my hand. I hadn't then. Now I did.

No wonder Ichiro's uncle had been glad to kill for this. No wonder it woke demons wherever we went.

In my pocket I had something better than freedom. Something that could make me a legend. Something that could turn me into the greatest ninja who ever lived.

Now I knew what I was holding.

Power.

EIGHTEEN

Whatever Tosabo's arrangements were, they seemed to be taking some time.

"We could go," Saiko said quietly as she sat beside me. "Couldn't we?" She didn't do anything so obvious as nod at the main gate, open in the morning sun. But I knew she was looking at it. So was I.

We were sitting in the courtyard, watching the business of the monastery going on around us. Monks hurried by to prayer or meditation or study or whatever it was monks did. Novices ran past in groups, shaven-headed boys younger than Ichiro. Servants carried brooms and bowls and baskets of laundry. No one took much notice of us.

Nothing stood between us and the gate. We could stroll calmly out. The gatekeeper would probably bow to Saiko as she went.

"I didn't know demons *had* souls," Ichiro said thoughtfully. He was kneeling comfortably on the ground, feet tucked under him, leaning back against a sunlit patch of wall. Shave his head and he'd look as if he belonged here.

"I don't think so," I answered Saiko softly, ignoring Ichiro's comment. "Over there."

I flicked my eyes toward a corner of the courtyard, and Saiko glanced there as well, without turning her head. A group of young monks had just stripped off their outer robes, piling them on the ground. They gathered up the wide legs of their trousers, tucking them into their belts to give themselves more freedom to move. Then they picked up wooden staffs that had been left leaning against a wall.

Apparently the monks here did more than pray and study and meditate.

They paired up, took their weapons, and began simple exercises of strike and parry, starting slow and then speeding up until the staffs whirled in their hands.

They were quite good. I felt my muscles flex and tense in sympathy, watching them. There were also enough of them to be a problem if we chose to leave now and they chose to object.

Of course, if Tosabo and his abbot were right, I could easily defeat every monk in this monastery. I could snap my fingers and they would all drop dead. I could bring the whole temple down, watch its walls crumble to dust.

But there were three wishes left, they'd thought. Perhaps four. I shouldn't waste any. I would have to take care and think hard about how to make the demon in my pocket best serve me.

Besides, now I could see Tosabo—where had he come

from, exactly?—walking past the monks and pausing to watch as a pair finished up their exercises and began to spar in earnest.

Tosabo lowered a pack that he held over one shoulder to the ground. He stood with his arms crossed, and the patience was suddenly gone from his face. Then he stepped forward and tapped the shorter of the two monks on the shoulder.

Both stopped at once and bowed, but Tosabo wasn't interested in a polite greeting. He gestured sharply, and the taller monk nodded and launched a kick at the old man's head that had me sure I'd see his ancient brains splattered across the dusty ground.

Instead, the younger monk was suddenly on his back, and Tosabo, his pack in his hand once more, was on his way across the courtyard to us before his opponent was able to pick himself painfully up.

"Come along then, children," Tosabo said cheerfully as he reached us. "Close your mouths, my dears; it's been a terrible spring for flies. The abbot has agreed. My penance is to escort you safely to your uncle's castle. A few of my friends will come along."

※　※　※

A few of Tosabo's friends turned out to be most of the monks who'd been sparring in the yard. Even a warlord's personal bodyguard would have hesitated to confront the hard-faced warrior monks riding alongside us.

I think Tosabo noticed a flash or two of white fur in the long grass. The fox was still with us. But he said nothing about her, and neither did I.

"Why do you . . ." I asked after we had stopped for the night. Tosabo was kneeling by the fire, his eyes closed, warm orange light dancing over his features.

Ichiro elbowed me in the ribs for interrupting a monk's meditation, but Tosabo merely opened his eyes and smiled. He smiled more than anyone I'd ever known.

"Do finish the question, my dear, so I can answer it."

Something in his eyes, dark and bright as the coals in the fire, made me think he knew just want I wanted to ask. And that irritated me. But clearly he was not going to offer me a thing unless I put my question into words.

I struggled for a while to find the right phrase, and then gave up. "Stay there. At the temple," I blurted. "You could be doing something *real*. In the world. You could—"

"Do finish your thought, my dear."

"Fight."

Tosabo nodded. "I do. I fight daily."

"I don't mean practice sparring," I said impatiently.

"Neither do I. I fight in deadly earnest. Anger, laziness, arrogance. Those are my enemies. Believe me, this is the hardest struggle I have ever faced." He laughed at the look I could feel on my face. "No, my dear. I know it is not your battle yet. But someday you'll turn that formidable will of yours on an enemy worthy of it. Meanwhile, let's try to keep your trinket from causing more harm, shall we? Ichiro, do you remember what I taught you while we were riding? Good. Excellent. Listen."

Ichiro joined Tosabo and some of the other monks as

they chanted, a slow, mesmerizing murmur that may have kept the demons at bay, or may have simply been designed to wash into my dreams like ocean waves and make me restless all night long.

But Ichiro's face, in the firelight—I had not seen him look so happy before.

I had never noticed the trace of anxiety that was always on his features until it was gone. With his eyes closed, his lips shaping the words of the mantra, he looked—peaceful.

It was strange. The serene look on his face did not make me feel exasperated, as Tosabo's smile did. But it did make me feel oddly lonely. As if Ichiro were gone from me.

And if he were, why should I care?

He'd been my target. Then he'd been my prisoner. Then, somehow or other, he'd become something between my client, my responsibility, and my friend.

But once I delivered him to his uncle's castle, our ways would part. Surely. In a day or two Ichiro and Saiko would be safe with their family behind castle walls, and I'd be— well. Where would I be?

Free to choose where I'd go. To choose what I'd do. To choose who I'd fight.

No, I would be more than free. I would be— invulnerable. I'd have safety wrapped around me like a cloak, power like a blade in my hand.

If, of course, Tosabo and his abbot had been right. If I really had a demon's soul at my command.

The monks seemed to have finished their chanting. Some lay down to sleep; others moved to the edge of the firelight, facing out, keeping guard. In the quiet, a tendril of doubt crept into my mind just as my hand crept inside my jacket. Could it really be true, this tale two old monks had spun me? They had seemed to know, and yet . . .

"When we get to our uncle's castle, I'm going to take a bath that will last for *days*." Saiko sighed. "And then I'll pluck my eyebrows. They must look like centipedes."

"I'm going to sleep," Ichiro said happily. "On a *bed*. With three quilts over me. No, four. No . . ."

And what about me? What would I do once we'd reached our destination?

I would become the best ninja the world had ever seen. *If* those two old monks had known what they had been talking about.

Inside my jacket, my fingers touched the pearl.

There had been that soldier under the tree, the samurai on the road. But perhaps the soldier had merely heard a badger rustling in the undergrowth. Perhaps the samurai, riding hard, simply hadn't heard Saiko's sneeze.

Saiko's face hardened as she stared into the fire. "And I'm going to make sure Uncle Hikosane gets what he deserves," she muttered.

"A very perilous thing, what we deserve," Tosabo remarked.

"He did bring the pearl to me," Ichiro objected. "You keep ignoring that, Saiko. We don't really know that he's as bad as you think."

Saiko snorted delicately. Only Saiko could do that. "We don't?"

No, we didn't really know. But perhaps we could find out.

Find out what Ichiro's uncle truly was. Find out whether Tosabo and his abbot were right.

I'd never trust my life to a blade whose edge I hadn't tested. If I were to rely on the pearl, I should know what it could do.

My hand slipped out of my jacket, clenched in a tight fist.

"My dear?" Tosabo, across the fire from me, sat suddenly upright. Then he was moving. But even Tosabo could not move faster than a wish.

And I *knew*.

The scene unfolded before my eyes, as if I were standing only a few feet away. Bodies of bandits and samurai lay on the bloody, trampled grass. One warlord with the Kashihara dragonfly on his breastplate stood disarmed in the center of a ring of swords. Another was before him, his shorter sword still thrust through his sash, his longer blade outstretched, its tip under the chin of the man who stood empty-handed before him.

I didn't need to see the two faces, so similar—the same thick eyebrows, the same strong noses and stubborn jaws—to realize that these men were brothers. The knowledge was already there, in my mind.

It was Ichiro and Saiko's father who stood with a blade to his throat. It was their uncle, Hikosane, who held the sword's hilt. What had Saiko said about him? That she had never seen a colder heart?

Then Hikosane drew back a step and let the bandits press in. His brother's back straightened. He looked Hikosane in the eye and threw himself forward.

There were yells; swords swung and flashed. But the weaponless man eluded every bandit there to seize the blade of his brother's sword with his bare hands. He had not been able to choose life, but he'd found the freedom to choose the death he wanted. In moments there was a sword through his throat, and his brother's hand was still on the hilt.

The vision was gone, and Tosabo's apprehensive and angry face was between me and the fire.

I heard a faint whimper from Ichiro. Saiko was sitting very still, her perfect face blank.

I'd wished for all of us to know the truth about Ichiro's uncle. The brother and sister must have seen the same vision I had. They must have watched their father die.

And now I knew that the monks had been right. This pearl could grant me—whatever I wanted.

I should have been triumphant. Instead, a harsh feeling swept over me, as though acid had washed through my veins. I remembered feeling cold up a tree and in the grass above a road, but this was worse. Something dark and horrible chuckled. I was fairly sure I was the only one who could hear it.

It took every ounce of my strength not to let myself shudder, not to let them all see what a wish had cost me.

"Stupid child. Stupid!" I thought Tosabo was about to slap me. "Do you have no sense? More importantly, do you have no soul?" The little old monk gripped my chin hard enough to hurt, forcing my head close to his so that he could peer into my eyes. I should have knocked him aside, but I was too shaken and startled to do it.

I felt his hand relax.

"I should take it from you," he muttered. "And I could, make no mistake—no, girl, I won't. The abbot wouldn't let me back in the monastery, for a start, and I owe him obedience, which is something you could stand to learn." He let my chin go. "Look at the pearl."

My fingers opened.

"Do you see? Look, child. Look at the gold."

The ring of gold around the pearl had been about as thick as my thumb when I had first examined it, back at the school. Now it was as narrow as my little finger.

"Once that gold is gone, the demon is free," Tosabo said, and there was anger in his voice, humming under tight control. "The demon you just felt—oh, yes, my dear, I know you did. Do you *want* to set that thing free on the world? On yourself? On your friends? I know what it is to hold a weapon in your hand. But do you have the strength to hold it and not use it? That is something we will see."

What good was a weapon if it was never used?

"Girl? Tell me you've heard me."

I blinked at Tosabo. Of course I'd heard him. Saiko had heard every word, too.

Ichiro had heard nothing. Unlike me, the boy did not let his pride keep him from shaking.

"He killed . . ." Ichiro whispered. "Uncle Hikosane killed . . ."

"Don't be a fool." Saiko's voice was sharp and clear,

and Ichiro flinched as if she'd flicked a whip at his face. "I told you he had a cold heart. I was wrong. He has no heart at all. And you might have seen it any time you looked at him. But you—you wanted to trust. To love, even." Her lip curled up in disgust. "To hope he'd be another father for us."

Tosabo moved from my side to put an arm around the boy's shoulders. He looked across the fire at Saiko with a frown. I looked at her as well, startled. There was nothing soft about Saiko now.

"Grief is a weakness," she told Ichiro. "Our father was not weak. He saw his own death coming, and he made sure who dealt the blow. You know why he did it. Father forced his own brother to kill him because his killer could not take the pearl. He knew that Hikosane would have no choice but to bring the jewel to you."

For no reason I could think of, I remembered the look in Saiko's eyes as I had peered, upside down, through a window and unexpectedly caught her gaze. I had not known what to make of her then. I didn't know now, as her words bored into Ichiro like the tip of a drill.

"We are not helpless children, Ichiro. Not anymore. Our father was willing to die to keep the pearl safe. Our uncle is willing to kill. You have to be willing to do both of those things now. It's the only way we can win."

"Enough," Tosabo said, even more sharply than he had spoken to me.

But there was one more thing that needed to be said. I rose and moved to Ichiro's other side. He had drawn his knees up and hidden his face against them, as if hiding from his sister's words, or from the truth that my wish had shown him.

"Ichiro." I laid a hand on the boy's shoulder. "I'll kill him for you. I promise."

※ ※ ※

The next day Tosabo rode close to Ichiro, talking to him softly. I was relieved. How to confront Ichiro's murderous uncle—that was something I could understand. How to comfort a stricken boy—that was beyond me.

I was busy with my own thoughts, in any case, and rarely rode close enough to hear what they were saying, though I did notice Saiko interrupting more than once. Ichiro would answer her politely and then return his attention to Tosabo without truly seeming to notice that his sister was there.

So I should not have been so surprised, perhaps, by what Ichiro said when he turned to his sister and me. It was late afternoon and the three of us stood on a hill overlooking the castle town of Kashihara Yoshisane.

The road we had been following meandered down the hill, crossed a broad, flat river, and led through the town's main gate. Tosabo and his monks had bidden us good-bye, but for some reason they'd paused on horseback perhaps twenty yards away, in sight but too far to overhear.

I looked back a little uneasily. The warrior monks had been nothing but kind to us, but that did not change what they could do if they decided to stop being kind. Of course, I had something in my pocket that could tip the odds in our favor. And Tosabo knew it. Still, why did the monks seem as if they expected something to happen?

"What are they waiting for?" I muttered.

"For me," Ichiro answered.

I blinked and looked down at him. "What?"

"They're waiting for me," Ichiro explained. "I'm going back to the monastery with them."

Small and stubborn, he stood there with a smile exasperatingly like Tosabo's. Saiko stared at him as if he'd suddenly sprouted a second head or perhaps a tail. With exaggerated patience, as if her brother were much younger than he was, she pointed out that he was not a monk or even a novice—he was a warlord's son. Trained to fight and born to rule.

"What are you going to do in a monastery?" I asked in my turn. "Pray? All day long? What good will that do you, or anyone?"

"I'll find out," Ichiro said simply.

"But what about—" I stopped. It did not feel safe, especially after last night, to mention the pearl under the open sky.

"Our family!" Saiko finished for me. She seemed to be slowly realizing that her brother meant what he said. "Will you shame us all like this? What am I to tell Uncle Yoshisane?"

"Tell him where I am." Ichiro shrugged. "What shame is there in that?" But he looked at me as if he knew what I had been going to say.

"It's yours now," he said soberly. "And, Kata, I'm sorry. You saved my life, and I handed you such a burden in return."

He'd handed me a demon to do my bidding, and he was apologizing to me. And he still thought I'd been kneeling by his bed to rescue him, that night. Shame welled up in my mouth and shriveled my tongue.

Saiko hissed and turned away.

"But what about your—your uncle. The one who—" I could not say, *the one who hired me to kill you.*

"The one who killed our father!" Saiko turned back in a flutter of skirts and sleeves. "You'll leave me alone, Ichiro? Am I the only one who'll seek vengeance?"

"If you need to." Ichiro actually looked sorry for her. "But, sister, I truly don't think it will help."

"Help!" Saiko looked ready to slap him.

"What if your uncle—" I lowered my voice. "Gets what he wants?" I fought the urge to slip my hand inside my jacket and clutch the pearl tightly. "You could—I need—" These were not words that came easily to my tongue. "We ought to keep the pearl from him," I said tightly. I'd seen his face, the man who'd held a sword to his own brother's throat. And I knew that the power of the pearl was not something that should be handed to a man like that. "You could *help.*"

I couldn't say, *I need your help.* But perhaps I did.

He was nothing but a boy. Still, he was brave and loyal. And kind. Not a virtue I'd have thought much of, a week or two ago. But I might have been wrong.

Ichiro shrugged again.

"Uncle Hikosane's fate is his own. If he gets what he wants, maybe he'll be a better man. Maybe I'd be just as bad as he is, if the pearl were in my hands." His gaze was on my face, and the trust in it nearly knocked me speechless. "The pearl came to you, Kata. I think you are the right guardian for it. Do as Tosabo told us, please. Don't use it again. Keep it safe." He glanced over his shoulder at the waiting monks, then surprised me for a second time by flinging his arms tightly around me. "Thank you, Kata," he whispered. "For my life."

Saiko shrugged out of the embrace he gave her next. Then Ichiro was running back to the monks. Tosabo reached down and pulled the boy onto his horse behind him.

So it was Saiko and I who crossed the bridge, walking by bored soldiers, dodging carts piled high with bags of rice and barrels of wine, listening to the songs of women beating clothes clean on the rocks below. Together, the two of us entered the castle town.

NINETEEN

"Get back here!" Saiko whispered fiercely.

She pulled me around the corner of a stall selling rice wine. An instant later, I saw why.

He was riding down the street, rather too fast for the crowded town, and surrounded by a troop of samurai, each with the dragonfly emblazoned on his brightly lacquered armor. People scattered out of their way, two porters nearly losing the load they carried from a pole over their shoulders. A fan seller leaped for safety and dropped his basket, spilling his brightly colored wares into the dirt where they lay like trampled butterflies.

I'd last seen him in a vision. I'd hoped not to see him again.

"Uncle Hikosane," Saiko whispered.

She put her hands to her face, as if to shield herself from flying mud. The warlord and his samurai went thundering up the street toward the castle, strong and well defended on the crest of a hill.

So that put an end to any thought of simply knocking at the gate.

"What is he doing here?" Saiko whispered, anxiously.

"Looking for Ichiro, probably. Looking for you."

"But now—what will we do?"

The rice wine dealer was starting to glare at us. We were not buying, and yet we were blocking access to his stall. Luckily, a crowd of customers charged up just then, claiming his attention as we moved a few steps away.

"We'll have to make sure Hikosane doesn't see you, that's all," I said, keeping my voice low.

"We don't know how long he'll stay," Saiko protested. "We could wait until he leaves, but—"

She didn't need to finish the thought. We could not hide days, or weeks, with the pearl in my pocket, demons stirring, and Lord Hikosane's samurai roaming the town.

The drinkers were still clustered around the booth, complaining loudly.

"Mud all *over* my kimono, look."

"That's nothing. My *hair*! Look at my *hair*!"

"I nearly had to dive out of the way. Suppose I'd sprained my wrist?" fretted a lean, droopy youth, rubbing his fingers tenderly. "I could have *broken* something."

"Here, have another cup to get over the shock," suggested a plump man, his eyes gleaming with a touch of malice.

"Certainly *not!*" A bulky man with a harried look and a bold mustache snatched the pottery cup and drained the wine himself. "Trying to get him drunk won't make you the foremost performer at the castle tonight. Right, then. Is everyone here? Is everyone safe? Is everyone *sober*? If no one has more to complain about than a bit of mud, we're all well off. No, *not* another cup! You've got to sing tonight!" The sour-faced woman who'd been fussing about her hair set down her cup with a drawn-out sigh. "Chokei, settle up. Give the poor man a tip for putting up with the likes of this lot. Honest merchant of the elixir of heaven—" There were groans from the drinkers, and the plump man took a sip of his wine and burst into exaggerated coughing. "Kindly tell all of your customers that this ragtag band of drunken reprobates will perform the finest songs and stories tonight at the castle for the entertainment of the warlord Kashihara Yoshisane himself!"

So, they were actors. I saw Saiko draw herself aside, pulling in her skirts to avoid contamination. She'd probably never been close enough to touch riverbank dwellers like these in her life.

"To the inn," the mustached man insisted. "No, I said no more! Hurry along, we've got three hours or so to make ourselves presentable. And that's barely enough time for Hideo to comb his hair." He gave the sake dealer an elegant bow of thanks and herded his troupe along the street.

My eyes met Saiko's, and we both nodded. Together we started off after them.

         🦋 🦋 🦋

Three hours later, you would not have known them. The harridan who'd shrieked about her hair looked as prim as Saiko, in a pale gold kimono; the plump man who'd tried to get his colleague drunk looked as solemn as a tax collector. The mustached leader had on a fine blue robe and a samurai's swagger, and he kept a hand on the elbow of the lean young man, who was humming and seemed to be paying no attention to anything that went on around him.

They were all much too busy thinking about their upcoming performance to notice two girls trailing them from their inn to the castle gates.

It had taken most of the three hours to find Saiko a kimono. She was fussy, and I wasn't willing to spend every one of the gold coins I'd stolen from Commander Otani. It had not been wise of him to leave a bag of looted treasure lying on the floor of the cave as we were talking. And he'd been quite right that I was in the wrong profession if stealing bothered me. Fortunately, I'd tucked the gold coins into one of the small and secret pockets along the hem of my jacket, so they had not been lost with the rest of our money when I'd left my pack behind in Okui's house.

After Saiko had rejected the first twelve kimonos, I'd lost patience and gone to wait under a tree, whittling sticks into slivers with my knife until she finally chose a robe of cheap, thin silk, dyed orange-red and embroidered with black diamonds. Once she had it on, it contrived to look showy rather than garish. Our leftover copper coins from Ryoichi's villagers had been spent on camellia oil for her hair, rice powder for her face, and safflower paste for her lips.

She should have looked like a child playing with her mother's clothes. But somehow, she looked—well, if not elegant, at least interesting. Like someone who might be allowed through the castle gates if she happened to come along behind a troupe of entertainers.

When we reached the gates, I moved away from her. She might have looked the part of a singer or a courtesan or both, but I did not.

Luckily, a band of samurai had just dismounted. I moved over toward them and grabbed the reins of a black mare with a nose as white as if she'd dipped it in paint. My hair was hidden under a hood, and hopefully I'd seem just another stable boy, unworthy of anybody's notice.

Saiko glanced behind her, and for one quick moment, our gazes met. She lifted a hand to her throat to touch the necklace that hung there.

It was a simple piece, a white pearl inside a ring of gold, hung on a black silk cord. But it would surely catch the eye of her uncle Yoshisane. It was more than an artifact of power, now. It was our passport to her uncle's notice. All she needed to do, once inside the castle, was to get herself into his line of sight.

It only lasted a moment, the look that passed between us. But it said all that needed to be said.

I still didn't like her—much. She was not particularly fond of me. But I trusted her to do her job, and she knew I'd do mine.

At least for this brief mission, she was a ninja after all. Like me.

When a hand in a heavy leather-and-iron gauntlet fell on my shoulder, and a voice bellowed, "What are you doing with my horse, boy?" she didn't even turn her head, but swept through the gates right behind the troupe of actors, leaving me behind.

The hand spun me around, and I lost my grip on the mare's reins and nearly my balance as well. "Only taking her to the stables, please, master," I whined, cringing.

My gaze went up to his face, and I felt my head jerk back a little in shock. Something soft—my hood—slithered down the back of my neck.

"So Yoshisane has stable *girls* looking after the horses now?" bellowed the samurai who had ahold of my shoulder. He seemed twice my height, was certainly twice my weight, and had the dragonfly on the breastplate of his armor. And half of his right ear was missing.

"Oh, master, please," I whimpered, hiding my dismay. "There's a boy, he works in the stables. Please, have mercy. I only wanted a word with him. He promised me—" And I cast a pitiful glance downward at my belly, hoping Daigoro would take the hint.

Of all the horses here, I'd had the bad luck to pick the one belonging to the man who'd chased me across a mountain range. Lord Hikosane's trusted retainer, the one Saiko had called his loyal dog.

"*You?*" Daigoro shouted, and I caught a waft of sour rice wine on his breath. "I doubt it, I very much doubt it. The stable boys have *pigs* if they're that desperate!" By now he had collected quite a crowd, and he looked around proudly as they laughed and I writhed in mock humiliation.

"Why are my retainers making a display of themselves at the castle gates?" asked a smooth and level voice behind me.

I was alarmed by the way the man holding me and all his laughing comrades fell instantly silent. Daigoro was a bully, and stupid to boot. Whoever *he* was afraid of might be trouble for me.

"Forgive me, my lord," he stammered. "I caught this little thief trying to steal my horse!" And he gave me a shove, so that I fell at his warlord's feet.

I looked up into the face of Kashihara Hikosane.

The man barely glanced at me. "And don't you know what to do with a thief?" the warlord said impatiently. "Throw it in the moat and waste no more time."

But the moat was not where I'd been planning to end up. It was still broad daylight. I could hardly swim across the water and scale the castle walls with the whole town looking on.

Daigoro seized my arm and yanked me up.

Well, if it was a thief they wanted . . .

Every kind of armor has joints built in, or the warrior would be unable to move. If that warrior is going to be riding a horse, the joints at the crotch must be generous. So that's where I landed my best kick.

As Daigoro folded in two and let go of my arm, Lord Hikosane reached for my hair. I dodged his hand, seized the jade-and-gold earring in his ear, and yanked. Now he and his loyal retainer would match.

Hikosane roared with pain and surprise, and I darted downhill toward the town, clutching my handful of bloody gold. They were all so shocked that I actually had to slip and let myself fall to give them time to catch me.

A horse thief they might have tossed in the moat to drown. A hellion who'd ripped open a warlord's ear—for her they had different plans. So I was told at length, before being dragged inside the gate, manhandled down a flight of stone stairs, stripped of my weapons, and tossed into a tiny cell. The door clanged shut, a bar slammed down across it, and footsteps clattered up the stairs.

Well, at least I was inside the castle.

I wiped my bloody nose on my shoulder and set about getting my hands free. That took longer than I would have liked. Daigoro had been the one to tie them behind me, and he'd done it much too tightly. If they'd left me like that all night, I'd have been a cripple by morning.

I wondered how Saiko was managing.

By the time I had the ropes off, both wrists were bleeding and I had to spend time I didn't have to stretch and massage my fingers. I couldn't rush it, though. I needed my hands in working order for the next thing I had to do.

Two choices now: the door or the stinking hole in the floor. I pried up the grate to take a look, but the smell nearly made me throw up, and the hole was narrower than my shoulders. I wasn't that desperate yet.

So, the door.

Not a simple latch, which would have taken me half a minute. Through the crack between the door and its frame, I could see the width of the wooden bar that held it closed. Thicker than my wrist, and heavy as well.

They'd taken my knife, but hadn't bothered to search me carefully enough to find the length of cord around my waist or the slender steel rod sewn into my right sleeve. One end was pointed and as sharp as a needle. The other was bent into a hook.

The rod fit neatly through the crack between the door and its frame. With the hooked end, I was able to draw the cord into a loop around the right end of the bar. Then I looped the free end of the cord around the bar's left end. With my sleeve wrapped around my fingers, so that the narrow cord would not cut the skin, I pulled gently and steadily upward. The bar came out with no trouble, and I eased the door open with my shoulder.

Once I was outside the cell, I set the bar back down into its rests, hoping to make it look as if I'd simply vanished. By the next morning, they'd be saying I was a demon. Soon the story would be that I'd bitten off Lord Hikosane's ear and flown away.

If they knew demons as I did, they would not speak of them so lightly.

There was no guard outside the door or at the top of the stairs. Perhaps they'd have set someone to watch a valued prisoner, but why bother for a girl thief? The cord went back around my waist, the rod into my sleeve. I did my best to clean all the blood off my chin and cheeks and hands, and pulled my loose hair over my face to cover what I hadn't been able to rub off. One good thing about dark clothing is that blood doesn't show.

In any castle, it's always fairly easy to find the kitchen.

Most of the servants are headed there. You simply pick one to follow. My first led me to the laundry, which was not helpful, but then I caught sight of a skinny boy lugging a heavy basket of radishes and greens across an inner courtyard. It wasn't hard to bump into him and knock him sprawling.

"Clumsy pig! Look what you've done!" he shouted.

"I'm sorry, so sorry," I whimpered, and dropped down to crawl after an errant radish. "I'll help. I'm sorry. I didn't mean to!" We scooped up the slightly bruised vegetables and piled them back into the basket. "Let me," I panted, and seized one of the handles. "You take that one."

He only grunted, but he was glad enough of the help, and it gave me an excellent excuse to enter the kitchen.

There, everyone was too busy to notice me at all. Fish were being skinned and boned by knives far deadlier than anything in Madame Chiyome's armory. Rice was steaming and bear paws soaked in honey were simmering. And apparently the pitchers of rice wine could not be filled fast enough.

When a maid thumped a full one down on the table, I snatched it up. By the time she turned her head to look for it, I was following two more servants back outside the kitchen and across a courtyard to the mansion and its banquet chamber.

The guests were all kneeling around low tables or leaning back on bright cushions. Servants knelt to fill wine cups and offer trays of sharp little pickles, or cakes oozing sweet bean paste, or sliced fish arranged to look like flowers in full bloom.

It was not easy to spot Lord Yoshisane through the crowd. Did he look like his two brothers, the ones I'd seen in the vision? I could not be sure. As I knelt to pour wine into cups thrust toward me, I sent my gaze darting about the room.

The music that had been dancing over our heads finished with a sweet swirl of notes, and I saw the tall young man from the actors' troupe take his wooden flute from his lips and bow humbly before a man wearing a white sleeveless robe over a long black kimono. On the white silk, a silver dragonfly fluttered its wings with the man's every breath.

A hand in a brown sleeve thrust a cup at me, and I splashed the wine in carelessly, my eyes on the man in black. Some of the pale liquid sloshed over the rim.

"Forgive me, master," I whispered, cringing. Stupid and careless of me. Now the samurai, whoever he was, would probably kick me. It wouldn't be in character for me to dodge, and certainly not to break his leg.

But there was something odd about that sake. Instead of dripping off the man's hand, the liquid began to bubble on his skin. It sizzled like water on a hot pan, and then vanished into the air with a little plume of steam.

As I stared, not quite believing my eyes, the man whose sake I'd spilled, instead of kicking me, reached over to take a firm grasp on my hair.

I gasped. His hand was hot, and the skin on the back of my neck ached as it would after a long day in the sun.

He had a bloodstained bandage on one ear.

Frowning, he turned my head slowly from side to side,

as if he were studying my face or the arrangement of my hair. His eyes were black, like any human eyes, but something red flickered over their surface, a reflection of flame. Something inside him was burning.

I'd spilled sake on Saiko's uncle. And Saiko had been wrong about him. The problem wasn't that he had no heart. The truth was, he had no soul—at least, no human soul.

Kashihara Hikosane was a demon.

I'd have to kill him. It was my only chance. But his own samurai were seated all around him. I might stab him through the heart with my sharp steel rod or the knife I'd stolen from the kitchen and hidden in my sleeve, but what were my chances of getting out of the room afterward?

Not good.

Lord Hikosane's hand tightened at the back of my neck, and I felt the skin there about to burn. Then something across the room seemed to catch his attention. I strained my eyes sideways and saw that he was looking at a man wearing a black kimono, and at a girl in a bright orange-red robe kneeling at his feet.

Hikosane rose, flinging me aside harder than should have been possible, so that I tumbled across the floor, sprawling in a litter of broken pottery and spilt rice wine. He stood up and took a step toward Saiko.

He did it clumsily, as though walking were something he was not used to doing.

I rolled to my knees, drew my kitchen knife from my sleeve, and threw it. But it was not balanced like the throwing knife I was used to, the one Hikosane's men had taken from me, and my aim was off. The knife sang through the air inches from Lord Hikosane's head and forced two guests behind him to dodge, before it tore through a paper screen and vanished.

"Saiko!" I shouted, over the panic that was starting to fill the hall. "Don't let him touch you!"

Good advice. Hikosane had flinched from my knife, stumbled, and fallen. Where his hands touched the polished bamboo slats of the floor, two black, smoldering patches appeared. Whatever was inside him was coming to the surface, his human façade burning away like a wisp of silk in the fire.

Saiko screamed and scrambled back as the demon that had once been her uncle heaved himself up and reached for her throat. Or, rather, for the necklace hanging there.

Hikosane's neck was lengthening. His hair was falling out. All around, people were screaming, cursing, running, crying. No one had any weapons, of course; no one would have insulted Lord Yoshisane by coming armed into his banquet hall.

Someone tripped over me and fell, headlong, while I sat on the floor, staring openmouthed, as if I had never seen a demon before. But this one—this one was worse than all the rest.

A monstrous snakelike creature writhed out of Lord Hikosane's kimono, leaving a puddle of brown silk on the floor. A mouth gaped; yellow fangs seemed to grow by the second. I'd wrestled a giant centipede, I'd punched a double-mouthed woman in the teeth, I'd fought off a nue—but this? I'd never been trained to fight a snake three times as large as me.

Lord Yoshisane had staggered to his feet and was shouting for his men. Armed soldiers poured into the room. Arrows flew at the demon, but they burst into flame in midair.

Bamboo, teak, paper, lacquer—this banquet hall would be burning like a torch within a moment.

My knife was gone. My garrote was useless. The steel rod in my sleeve would do as much damage to this creature as a mosquito's bite. But what about fire? Could I fight this demon with its own weapon?

I leaped up and ran, heading for a lantern hanging from a wall as the demon reared up to strike at Saiko. She dodged and screamed. The snake snarled, a sound that might have been a laugh.

Lord Yoshisane shouted again.

My hand closed around the lantern.

The snake's tail lashed, toppling Lord Yoshisane like a doll.

I flung the lantern at the demon's head, splattering burning oil onto its face.

The snake hissed, snapping its head around to look at me and giving Saiko a few seconds to back away. A black tongue flickered from its mouth, licking hungrily at the flames.

Well, perhaps fire was not the right weapon . . .

"Kata!" Saiko shrieked. "Catch!"

And she flung the pearl at me. Even the demon was

startled, I think. It snapped at the jewel in midair, like a dog trying to catch a bothersome wasp, but it missed.

Before my hand had even closed around the pearl, I'd wished.

TWENTY

Mist swirled around me and knit itself into a shape. It was hard to look at, brighter than fire. I shielded my eyes and squeezed them closed, but the light from the thing still burned my skin.

The snake-demon squealed in panic.

I heard words, perhaps not with my ears. They were slick and oily, seeming to slide into my mind, chuckling with delight at their own evil.

Ah, it's been a long time. Laughter that made me cringe. *I haven't had a good fight in too many years. Shall I take care of this snakeling for you?*

I managed to nod, my eyes still shut tight.

Easily done. And then, little one, we'll see . . .

There was a shriek, and a grinding, splintering crash.

Now look. I will not harm your eyes.

Cautiously I peeled my hand away from my face and opened my eyes.

He was beautiful, my demon. He had soft, shadowy wings and a samurai's two swords. He had a cat's sleepy golden eyes. He had Ryoichi's soft, gentle face.

Ryoichi's face?

And then the demon laughed, again, and flesh peeled and fell from the face to reveal moldy bone underneath. I bit back my scream. I would not cower. If this thing wanted my soul, it would take it. But it would not have my honor as well.

I heard a voice in my head again, and it was not the demon's. It was an instructor's from long ago, a man whose name I'd never known.

Never throw your last knife.

With the hand that was not holding a pearl on a chain, I reached inside my jacket to draw the second knife I'd stolen from the kitchen. The skull facing me grinned even wider. What did I think I'd do to a demon like this with a knife meant for scaling fish?

I turned the knife toward myself, resting the point just below my breastbone, where the ribs came together.

Was it possible that the empty eye sockets of the skull had widened?

One quick thrust. That would be all it would take.

When a samurai took the honorable path to ending his own life, a companion usually stood by with a sword to quickly strike off his head. But a ninja was not likely to have a friend close by to end her suffering. I'd have to wait out the minutes until my soul escaped with my blood.

But once my soul was in the underworld, I doubted

that any demon could fetch it back. From the way this one was hesitating, it doubted as well.

Oh, no, not yet, the skull said, grinning at me.

The face rebuilt itself, and to my shame, I flinched. My hand twitched, the knife pulled away from my skin, and I took a step back without realizing it. When my foot came down on a chunk of broken pottery, I fell in a clumsy heap.

Now it was Madame who peered down at me, disgust on her face. She tipped her head to one side, considering what to do with such a useless girl. *Not yet*, she told me. *Your soul . . . it isn't quite finished. I look forward to seeing what becomes of it.*

And she was gone. I sat there, dazed, in the middle of a ruined banquet hall, my knife in one hand, a pearl necklace in the other. I pulled the chain over my head and tucked the jewel away inside my jacket, fingering the thin gold ring.

Lord Yoshisane was getting unsteadily to his feet, holding up his black sleeve to blot the blood that was dripping down his cheek. On the other side of the room, Saiko, on the floor like me, pushed her hair back from her face and stared.

Between us lay the charred body of a man in a deep brown kimono, his soul devoured a long time ago.

※ ※ ※

It all took a considerable amount of explaining. Luckily that was Saiko's task, not mine. Lord Yoshisane, once he'd grasped that the demon who had so rudely interrupted his banquet was truly gone, had quickly and quietly taken charge. His startled guests were bidden farewell. His brother's body, what was left of it, was removed. Servants were ordered to set the hall to rights. Saiko was whisked away to make it clear to him why we were in his castle, how we had gotten here, why his family treasure was in the possession of a young, grubby, tired, and female ninja, and incidentally, what had become of his nephew.

I was brought to another room to wait.

This time I was not in a cell. I had a small, windowless room to myself. There were fresh, clean mats on the floor and an elegant piece of calligraphy on a wall. But I thought that, if I tried to leave, I was likely to find out that this was also a prison.

I could have gotten out anyway. I'd been twelve years old the last time a lock had defeated me. But I found I didn't want to try. I had been running for—how long? It was impossible to remember. Since the night I'd crept into Ichiro's room and knelt by his bed with a knife?

Or since a time long before that?

Enough. I'd reached my destination. I thought I would stay here for at least a few hours.

Besides, servants kept entering and bowing and leaving food on the low table beside me, and I discovered that I was ravenous. Confronting a demon, or two, seemed to leave me shaky and hollow inside. I ate salmon and sea bream with sharp ginger, rice, pickles and radishes, melon and pear and fried cakes both sweet and savory. I drank cup after cup of tea, but let the wine sit untouched. I might need my wits about me later.

It turned out that my wits did not help me much.

I had lifted the last sweet cake to my lips when the door slid open and Lord Yoshisane came in. Behind him was Madame Chiyome.

The cake plopped back to the plate, but my chopsticks stayed poised in midair.

Like a pot with a tight lid, Madame looked serene but she was bubbling with rage. I could tell by looking at her smile. And there was no one in the room but me to be her target.

"Bow, child," she said mildly. "This lord will think I have taught you no manners."

I dropped my chopsticks and pressed my face to the mat, although every inch of skin on my back prickled as I made myself so vulnerable.

Then I rose to my knees as Lord Yoshisane settled himself on the mat beside the table and gestured for Madame to do the same.

One exit to the room, behind him. I doubted I could reach it. And even if I did, what then? How far would I get in a castle where every servant and soldier and samurai would be hunting me down?

If you get free, don't come back, Masako had told me. I'd done the first, but not the second. I'd be back at the school by nightfall. And I'd never get a second chance to escape. Madame would see to that.

She was a ninja, too.

"My niece, Saiko, has told me a remarkable story," Lord Yoshisane was saying politely to Madame. "Wine? Please, honor me by tasting a little." Madame took the cup with her eyes still on me. "It is, hmmm, surprising that these two were able to come so far, and bearing what they have borne. Two girls. I would not have thought it possible." He poured his own wine and rolled the small, smooth cup gently between his palms. "Some of the credit must go to their teacher, of course." He gave Madame a little bow. "Still, I must say it again. Remarkable."

He set the cup down without sipping from it and turned to me. "You could, of course, simply hand the pearl back to me. One little cut with a knife, and you would be free of the burden. But I don't imagine that would be to your liking. No, I thought not."

"You could be made to, girl," Madame hissed suddenly, leaning forward, her eyes as cold and unblinking as a snake's.

Yes, I could be made to hand the pearl over. I had no doubt. If Madame preferred not to kill me herself, she had no shortage of hired knives. It could be quick if she felt merciful.

I could not remember a time when Madame had felt merciful.

"I would not dream of putting you to such trouble simply to retrieve a family bauble," Yoshisane told her politely. "No, indeed. Instead, allow me to take a problem off your hands. How much would you ask for such a rebellious and troublesome agent?"

Madame was more startled than I was.

"You wish to hire Kata? For a mission?" Madame covered the surprise on her face with a smile. "Well, she is one of my most skilled girls, of course, so the fee—"

"Of course," Yoshisane replied. "But—forgive me, you misunderstand. I do not wish to hire her. I wish to buy her. She would be permanently in my service."

"Well." Madame sipped rice wine and patted her lips dry. "Well. It's hard to estimate the value of a girl like Kata. Years of training, you know. She's been in my care since she could barely talk. More like a daughter of my own than a pupil. So difficult to put a price on that."

"All mothers, sadly, must part with their daughters one day," Yoshisane said with sympathy. "Even such a disobedient daughter as this one. She actually ran away from your house, did she not? After failing entirely in her first mission?"

"Failing?" Madame laughed. "To bring your cherished niece and nephew to safety? To protect them from every threat? You call that failure?" There was not the slightest hint in her voice or on her face that two of those threats had been in her pay and under her command.

"But it was not what she had been hired to do," Yoshisane pointed out. "If my brother was not unfortunately— mmm—unavailable, I believe you'd be returning his fee to him. Perhaps we should consider what he gave you to be a down payment on Kata's services to me."

More laughter. "I hardly think—"

"No," I whispered.

For the first time since they had started their bargaining, they both turned to look at me.

"You wish to return to the school?" Lord Yoshisane

asked, his eyebrows rising slightly.

"No." The word came from my mouth a second time, husky and faint, like the speech of a ghost.

I didn't want to go back, not at all. And here was Saiko's uncle, offering to keep me and the pearl I owned out of Madame's clutches. What kind of a fool would object to that?

If you get free, don't come back, Masako had said.

She had not said, *If you get free, stay free.*

But that might have been what she meant. And it was what I wanted.

Not to be bought or sold like a sack of rice. Not to be a knife in someone else's hand. To be free like a village with no warlord, like a band of thieves who rode where they chose. Perhaps even like a monk who had finally found a worthy opponent, even if that opponent was himself.

Madame's hand against my cheek knocked me sprawling. Before my head cleared, she had a handful of my hair and her face was inches from mine.

"Do you think you have a word to say here?" she hissed. Lord Yoshisane was courteously pretending that he could not see or hear us. "You are worth something, girl. But that does not make you *important*." She dropped her voice even further. "And every word out of your mouth now lowers your value. So let there be no more."

She wrung my hair tightly and let me go.

"A very troublesome daughter," Yoshisane commiserated. "Do let me relieve you of such an encumbrance."

"I will not deny that she needs a firm hand." Madame

smiled graciously. "And that will of hers—exasperating, to be sure, but such an asset on a mission. As you know yourself, Lord Yoshisane. Or she would not be sitting here."

I knelt, staring numbly at the hem of Yoshisane's robe while they bargained. The silk had a subtle pattern of diamonds within diamonds woven into the cloth itself. When they were done at last, Madame left the room on Yoshisane's heels, nearly preening herself with pride and pleasure. They both walked past me without a glance.

I had value, certainly, as the heavy coins in Madame's purse proved. So did a finely crafted sword or a rare poison. Those things had no will, no mind, no heart. And clearly, neither should I.

The next cell they took me to in Lord Yoshisane's castle had a thick futon already unrolled on the floor, a soft silk quilt, and new clothes, since mine had all been taken from me.

Normally a ninja, locked up, would have several secret tools or weapons. But Madame, of course, had supervised the search, and Lord Yoshisane's men had taken every weapon I had left in my pockets. In fact, they had taken my pockets themselves, as well as the clothes they belonged to. It was the easiest way for Madame to make sure I was defenseless.

They'd only left me two things. One was the pin for my hair, after Madame had given the stick a quick twist to be sure it actually was a hairpin, and nothing deadlier.

The other was the necklace around my throat, with its single pearl in a ring of gold. Why would Lord Yoshisane bother taking that from me? He'd bought it, and me along with it. We both belonged to him now.

The room even had a window; they were that sure of me. After I'd put on the new trousers and jacket, I slid the screen open and looked out at the sunset, and then down onto a sheer stone wall that led to the moat below.

I turned my head and looked up toward the roof.

*　*　*

It was mildly unpleasant to be dangling by my hands from slick ceramic tiles above a long drop to a deep moat, but I was not there for long. With my bare toes on the edge of the wooden window shutter, I was able to give myself enough of a push to hook a heel over the roof's edge. Then it was easy enough to heave myself up onto the tiles and crawl over the roof's peak. The drop down to one of the inner courtyards was nowhere near as harrowing.

By the time I got to the castle's kitchen, there was only one servant still awake there. She was willing to take pity on me when I wept and whimpered that I'd gotten lost and my new mistress would surely beat me for taking so long to return to her. Through yawns, she told me which room to look for. I bowed in humble thanks, scurried out of the kitchen, and found a handy pile of firewood that gave me a boost back up onto the castle's roof.

I felt safer here, well away from the eyes of Lord Yoshisane or anyone who worked for him. It was easy enough to walk the roof tiles, imagining that I was following the servant's directions through the corridors below. When I found myself standing on top of the room I'd been searching for, I lay down and reached over the eaves. Sure enough, a window.

I longed for my knife or my sharp steel rod or anything that would have cut the paper screen silently. But since I had nothing, I fished in the darkness for a broken bit of roof tile and flung it hard at a nearby tree. As I'd hoped, the tree exploded with startled, squawking birds, and their racket covered the noise I made when I punched my fist through the window.

Saiko heard me, however, and was beside me as I swung in. "Kata, are you *mad*? What are you *doing*?"

"Looking for you, of course." I dropped to the floor.

"Why didn't you just come to the door?" she asked, bewildered. "Honestly, Kata, I think you *like* climbing over roofs and down walls."

"And he'd just let me wander around the castle, of course."

"Who would?" Saiko had been fumbling with a lamp. Now a spark had been struck and the wick was burning in its bowlful of oil, a tiny pool of brightness in the dark room.

"Your uncle." I snatched up that garish red-orange kimono and used it to cover the window, so our light would not be seen outdoors. "The one who locked us in?" I prompted, and Saiko only stared at me.

She stepped over to her door, slid it open and shut, and lifted her perfect eyebrows—she'd had a chance to pluck them. "Why would anyone lock me in?"

"Because they want us—want us to—" Thoughts were tangling in my head, words on my tongue. "To serve them. He *bought* me. Your uncle. From Madame. Saiko, he owns me now."

"And me as well." Saiko had knelt gracefully beside her futon and gestured for me to do the same. "He always did. Or

Uncle Hikosane owned me, or my father. Ichiro is the only boy, but I am the only girl. Do you know how many arguments I've listened to over who I'd marry? Whether they'd use me to turn an enemy into an ally, or an ally into family? Do you think any of them ever thought once of consulting me? Kata, listen." She leaned forward a little, and I saw a light in that lovely face I had never seen before.

"He owns you, but he *needs* you," she said, her voice low, her body tense as a bowstring. "He needs both of us. There are bandits in the hills. Lords on his borders who'd love to take his land and his peasants. The territory of two dead brothers to control. He needs what you can do for him. Information. Assassination. And I can help. Maybe I can't fight, but I can do other things. You would be surprised to know what I can do."

I heard Madame's voice in my head. *Do you know the right moment to peer out from behind a fan? Can you catch a man's attention with one glance? Could you keep his eyes on your smile and off your hands?*

"Think of it, Kata. He won't be able to do without us. He won't own us. We'll own *him*."

I shook my head.

"What?" She was all sweet concern. "Kata, this is the best either of us could hope for. What more could you want?"

"Freedom," I said weakly. "Don't you—Saiko, don't you want to choose? Who you'll fight, and when, and what you'll get when you win?"

She laughed. "Who gets to choose?"

I thought of Ryoichi. Of Otani, his smile flashing in the firelight. Of Tosabo.

"Oh, Kata." She might have read my mind. "Do you want

to be free to be a peasant in a hovel? A bandit in a cave? That's just the freedom to die." She lifted both arms, graceful as a dancer, and spread them out to the darkness around us. "You'll live in a castle. Have a warlord dancing to your whim. What better freedom is there than this?"

She'd made her choice, then. I made mine. I blew out the lamp and went swiftly to the window, pulling the kimono down.

"You're truly leaving?"

"I'm leaving."

"How will you get out?"

"What do you care?"

"Wait—no, Kata, wait. Listen. You don't have any tools. Are you going to climb the wall with your fingernails? *Listen.*" She was beside the window now, a gentle hand on my arm. "There's a door in the outer wall. No one knows. It leads to a tunnel under the moat. You can get out that way. You'll be safe."

"How do you know about it?" I asked suspiciously.

In the darkness, I heard her gentle laugh. "Ichiro and I played all over this castle as children. There's not an inch of it that I don't know. There's a shrine in the garden. The door is in the wall behind it. Covered in vines, but it's there; you'll see it. Good fortune, Kata. You'll need it."

I paused with one leg over the sill. "You'll need more than I will. Good fortune, Saiko."

TWENTY - ONE

From the rooftop, I could see the garden, gray and black in the moonlight. A pale glimmer was probably the shrine. I waited, stretched out flat on the tiles, long enough to be sure I'd meet no guards, and then I scrambled down and ran.

I ducked behind the shrine and whispered a quick prayer to whatever god lived in the small stone dwelling under the slanted, moss-covered roof. Although any god here would be a friend of the Kashihara family, and very unlikely to pay heed to me. The wall behind the little building was covered with trailing vines, just as Saiko had said. I ran my hands over it and found a long crack that led my fingers to a keyhole.

A keyhole? Saiko had not mentioned a key.

"There she is!"

I'd been so intent on finding the door that I'd forgotten to keep my ears open. Fool, fool, *fool*, many times over, but this was not the moment to curse myself, because three guards were outlined against the moonlight, coming toward me.

I threw myself down and scrambled away, hunched over like a monkey, my hands helping me along. They'd be looking for a girl running, not a low-to-the-ground shape more like a dog. I dove behind an artistic cluster of moss-covered boulders. But the stones would not hide me long. There was shouting. Every guard on patrol would be here any second.

"I'll get them off your trail," offered a soft voice behind me.

Twice in a few minutes I'd let something sneak up on me. I must have forgotten all my training. On my knees, I whirled, ready to fight, but the voice was familiar. And Saiko *hadn't* snuck up behind me. She must have left her room just after I had, and probably by the door. She'd been hidden in the shadow of the boulders all along, waiting for me.

"She's a ghost. Where did she go?" came a call from not far away.

"She's only hiding, idiot. Look over there."

"Lord Yoshisane said a gold coin, didn't he?"

"Not if we're fools enough to lose her. Go!"

Saiko and I knelt, still as two more boulders, while a soldier thundered by. When he was gone she spoke again.

"Give it to me, and I'll draw them off."

Cold licked along my bones.

"You sent them here," I growled.

"Of course I did. Give me the pearl, Kata. It's mine. My family's." Frustration was bubbling over in her voice. For the first time since I'd known her, every word wasn't polished and perfect. "I always knew our father would give it to Ichiro one day. He could see, anyone could see, how weak that boy is, but even so, he never once dreamed of giving the pearl to me. He never saw that I'm the one who truly knows how to use it. Let me have it, Kata. I need it. No one will be able to ignore me. No one will control my life but me. Not if I'm the one who holds the pearl."

She held out her hand, pale in the moonlight, waiting. "If you keep it, they'll never stop chasing you. You know it. Give it to me now, and escape."

"How can I escape?" I had one hand on the necklace around my throat. "You lied about the door. It's locked."

"I didn't lie. Look, can you see?" Something in her hand glinted silver in the moonlight. "The key. I'll trade it to you for the pearl. Hurry, Kata. Choose. They'll be back any second."

I'd been entirely wrong about her from the start. She may not have been able to scale a wall or throw a knife, but she *was* a ninja.

I slipped the necklace over my head and clutched it in one hand. "I need a knife," I told her.

Saiko held out a dagger. She kept a firm grip on the hilt. Oh, I could have taken it from her if I'd tried, but maybe this was better after all. I pressed the palm of my left hand down on the blade, felt it bite, and then gripped the pearl.

I squeezed; warm blood spread over my skin. Then I opened my hand and offered the bloody pearl to Saiko. "It's yours."

She snatched it. The key dropped into my hand.

"Count thirty, slow. Then run for the door." With a whisper of silk, she rose and was gone.

Did I trust her? Not an inch.

Did I do what she'd told me? Yes.

I counted *one* as I breathed out. *Two* as I breathed in. Before I'd gotten to five, I heard Saiko's voice. "Over here! Fools, this way! Don't lose her!"

When I'd reached thirty, I rose and made my way to the shrine. I didn't bother with a prayer this time.

"Turn around, girl."

Oh, not *now* . . .

I turned slowly to see a soldier, sword in hand, step out from the shadow of the shrine and walk toward me.

"I thought you might come back this way." Teeth gleamed briefly in the moonlight. "Lord Yoshisane wants you in one piece, so come quietly, now."

He was holding his sword carelessly, almost loosely. He saw no threat before him—just a girl, unarmed, alone.

He was not expecting the kick that caught him in the knee. He certainly wasn't expecting the next, the one that knocked this sword out of his hand.

Before the blade could hit the ground, I had my fingers around the hilt.

And it was as if the sword thought for itself. All those hours in the practice yard, all those dances of attack and parry, had been for this, so that my muscles would know what to do before my brain had to tell them.

Swing high—a feint. He dodged, but my sword was already there. The weapon had no weight at all in my hand.

It moved of its own will, and the man fell to his knees, clutching with both hands at the blood welling from a deep cut under his ribs.

It dripped black as oil over his fingers.

The soldier didn't call for help. He didn't dare. The tip of his own sword was at his throat.

For one long heartbeat, we stayed so, unmoving. All I had to do was flick my wrist, and he'd be dead.

All he had to do was shout, and I'd be a slave.

Madame would have killed the man without a second thought. So would Saiko.

And was that who I wanted to be? Madame? Saiko?

A deadly flower?

I made a decision then, with my eyes on the soldier's frightened face, fighting the eagerness of the blade in my hand. Whatever I was, whatever I became, the next person I killed would be *my* choice. That much I could promise Raku's spirit. I wouldn't kill strangers, random targets, sleeping boys, girls I'd grown up with. If I killed again—and I probably would—it would be someone I had chosen to die.

I tossed the sword in the air, caught it with a new grip on the hilt, and before the kneeling man could react, hit him neatly on the temple, just where the skull is thinnest. He keeled over quietly, and I turned back to the door. The crack—there. The lock. The keyhole.

Had Saiko been lying about the key? She had not. It took all my strength to turn it, and the old lock groaned as if it disliked being awakened in the dead of night, but it did open. I put my shoulder to the door and shoved with all my strength. It yielded, inch by inch. Inside, I saw a stone staircase, descending into sooty blackness.

Before I stepped onto the first stair, I looked back down at the man I'd defeated. He was lying motionless on the ground. When I held my breath, I could hear his.

How badly had I hurt him? I wasn't sure. But I knew he was bleeding into the soft moss.

How much blood had he lost already?

Most likely someone would find him before he bled to death. This garden was swarming with Lord Yoshisane's retainers. He'd be found.

Most likely.

He was my enemy. I had no obligation to help him, or to show him more mercy than I already had.

Then why wasn't I already shutting this door behind me?

I cursed Saiko, the Kashihara family, their pearl, and everything that had brought me to this pass. And I shouted, in as deep a voice as I could manage, "Over here! I have her!"

Then I dragged the door shut behind me.

The blackness that closed around me felt like a living thing. I was wrapped in its arms; I felt it nuzzle my skin.

I whispered a thank-you to Madame and her instructors for all the times they'd made me walk a tightrope blindfolded or fight with a scarf over my eyes. I felt with my toes for the edge of each step—twenty of them—and eased my way down, careful not to fall and gut myself with the soldier's sword, still in my hand. It felt as if, at any moment, I'd be knocking on the gate of Yama, the lord of the underworld. Perhaps I should ask him for a cup of tea.

When at last there were no more steps, I inched my way along a passage, brushing my fingertips against a wall to guide me. The stones oozed moisture under my touch; drops fell from the ceiling and struck my head like hammers, astonishing in their weight and force and coldness. I was under the moat now. Above me were tons and tons of cold black water. One crack, one leak, and—

Don't think about that.

I splashed through puddles. Other things splashed, too. Some of them scuttled or skittered over my bare feet.

Don't think about that either.

After an eternity, or perhaps two, my toe bumped into something. I groped, felt another set of stairs, and went up cautiously, counting twenty steps. Then I put a hand out to touch the door ahead of me.

The same key worked here, I was glad to discover. I slid it into the lock, but before I turned it, I hesitated.

Lord Yoshisane's secret door was not as secret as he thought. Saiko knew about it. And she knew I'd gone through it.

Saiko, the one who'd trapped me so neatly, forcing me to hand the pearl to her. Saiko, the one who, by Madame's word, had it in her to become a ninja every warlord in this land would fear.

Saiko, the one I had underestimated day after day.

There in the clammy darkness, I thought of the journey we had made together. Saiko had rescued me from a crawling, ravenous thing that had burst through a trapdoor.

She had helped us get past bandits. She had saved me from a double-mouthed woman.

Saved *me*? Or saved the pearl I'd had in my pocket?

Saiko had sneezed when her uncle's samurai were mere feet away. Had she wanted to catch their attention, to draw them into a fight with me? If they'd killed me, she could have snatched a chance to take the pearl for her own.

When I'd been trapped in knee-high mud, Saiko had tried to help me. She'd told me to give her my jacket so that she could use it to pull me out. My jacket with the pearl tied safely inside. If I'd done as she said, would my bones now be sinking slowly down into that mud?

And was I going to trust Saiko's escape route? Was I going to open this door?

Not without checking first. I lay flat to put my ear next to the crack at the bottom of the door and listened.

For a while I heard nothing but the sound of my own heartbeat against the slimy, muddy stones. And then a sigh. And then a rustle, as of dried grass beneath the feet of a man impatiently shifting his weight. And a grunt, demanding silence. Too late.

Twenty steps down. Hurry through the dank tunnel as quickly as possible while carrying a piece of razor-sharp metal. Twenty steps up. I listened at the other door. No one there, as far as I could tell. When I eased it open, the body of the man I'd defeated was gone. His friends, it seemed, had found him.

No one saw me creep through the gardens and make

my way to the stable. No one saw me find a quiet spot in a storeroom full of harness and tack. Plenty of people saw me leave, the next morning, when the gates were open. But none of them remembered a plain servant girl lugging a bundle of laundry to the river. None of them ever saw her again, either.

TWENTY - TWO

Some time later, that same girl sat on a stone by a stretch of empty roadside, looking over fields of rice to the mountains that lay beyond.

It had been a strange feeling, the one that had come over me as I'd slipped unnoticed out of Kashihara Yoshisane's town. I'd felt something like it before, when I'd been alone with a warlord's sleeping mansion at my mercy.

During that first mission, I had been giddy, floating on my own excitement. Once I crossed the bridge that led out of the castle town, I felt that same giddiness bubbling up inside my heart—but something serious overlaid it and kept me from laughing.

I was free. I was also alone, unarmed, without so much as a lockpick to my name. I had not even kept the young soldier's sword, since I'd had nowhere to hide it under the clothes of a skinny young washer-girl. So I'd reluctantly left it behind, thrust deep into a bale of hay where it would be a considerable surprise to a stable boy one day.

No weapons. No food. No money. I had nothing at all, except my clothes, my training, and a choice to make.

I would not be returning to Madame Chiyome. Masako had known, better than I did myself, what I wanted most of all. I'd keep my word to her. Once free, I'd stay free.

The temple would have taken me in, no doubt. Ichiro would have been glad to see me. Tosabo might even have had something to teach me. But his way of fighting—it was not my way.

Ryoichi's village might have welcomed me. They'd been kind to me, even willing to face armed bandits for my sake. And I'd been born in a place much like that. But Madame had taken me from that world. How could I fit back into it now, after all I had learned and done?

Otani's bandits, then? I could ride with them, and my pockets would grow heavy with other men's treasure. I would have comrades, if not exactly friends.

The bushes across the road rustled and the white fox poked her nose out between the leaves. She slipped from the undergrowth and sat on the path, watching me. And then she changed.

"Have you made your choice?" asked the beautiful woman in the snow-white kimono. And I knew she was not speaking of the direction my next step would take me.

I put up a hand to the pin that held back my hair.

My instructors at Madame Chiyome's school had been right. Your enemies will take your weapons, your lockpicks, even your clothes—but they will not bother with your hair ornaments.

While Saiko had been shopping for her kimono, I'd whiled away the time by making a new hairpin from one of the sticks I'd whittled to a point. I'd used a bit of pine sap, sticky as glue, to attach the pearl. More sap, mixed with dirt, had dulled the milky sheen of the jewel and the glimmer of the gold. The new pin had been in my hair since I'd walked into Kashihara Yoshisane's castle.

My old hairpin, with its sharp and hidden blade, had been tucked into a pocket of my jacket and had been taken, along with my other tools, when Lord Yoshisane's men had searched me. But they hadn't taken the new pin, and they hadn't taken my necklace.

For that necklace, I'd used a white pebble from the river where I had first met the ghost. It had made an excellent substitute for the pearl. While Saiko had occupied herself with camellia oil and safflower paste, I'd found a jeweler who was willing to take one of Otani's gold coins for payment and beat a second into a ring to wrap around the white stone.

How long would it be before Saiko yielded to the temptation and tried to make a wish? Until then, she'd have no idea that the pearl I'd handed so reluctantly to her was a fake.

Now, facing the fox woman, I slid the pin from my hair. A soft sound above, like a hundred indrawn breaths, caught my ear, and I looked up to see tengu clustered on the branches overhead, craning their necks and tipping their heads to catch a glimpse of the pearl as I held it in my hand.

"Do you have a knife?" I asked.

Whether I went to a village or a temple or a bandit's cave, I could not go there with this pearl in my possession, drawing every restless demon and hungry ghost after me.

But I couldn't simply cast it away. Someone like Hikosane might be the one to pick it up. Or someone like Saiko.

The fox-woman had guided us out of Lord Hikosane's garden. She'd kept her word in the mountains and saved us from the nue. If she'd done all this merely in order to fool me into handing over the pearl—well, then it had worked.

She was of the spirit world, after all. She knew the ways of gods and ghosts and bakemono. She'd be a better guardian for the pearl than I could ever be.

But she shook her head. She had no knife.

Well, a sharp rock, then. I found one at my feet, picked it up, and held the jagged edge to my palm. It would not take much to reopen the cut I'd made when I'd given Saiko the false pearl.

"No." The fox-woman reached out and took the rock gently from me.

Startled, I looked up at her. "But I can't give it to you unless I . . ."

Her smile this time was kind. It didn't seem to hide a snarl behind it.

"Don't give it to me at all," she said. "It's yours."

"But I don't—I don't want it." I held it out to her again. What kind of freedom would that be, if I escaped from

Madame Chiyome and Lord Yoshisane and Saiko, but kept a demon in my pocket, hungrily eyeing my soul?

"I know you don't want it. And that's why I won't take it." It took me a moment to recognize the look in her eyes—it was pity. It had been so long since I had seen that in anyone's face.

"I was sent to be sure the pearl found its true owner at last," she went on. "I wasn't sure about you, so I stayed close to watch. And now I know. You're the one to hold it, Kata. It must stay with you."

"Sent?" I asked stupidly, still holding out the hairpin with the pearl attached.

"We all serve some master, no matter how free we may be," she said softly, and then she changed. A white fox dashed away into the undergrowth, a cloud of dark wings darted off between the trees, and I was left alone, holding a demon's soul between my fingers.

I was the right one? What did that mean? Who had decided? And more importantly, what was I supposed to do with the pearl? Use it? Destroy it? Keep it safe forever?

I was certain about only one thing: with this burden to carry, I could not find a home in a warlord's castle or a bandit's cave, in a temple or a village. So it seemed I'd have to be a ninja after all. And in my pocket I had something that could turn me into the greatest ninja this land had ever seen.

Or that could devour my soul.

Faint and far above, something laughed as I tucked the pearl safely inside my jacket and turned my face toward the mountain peaks.

Author's Note

Ninjas

In the feudal age of Japan, when most of the power lay with military leaders, the ideal warrior was the samurai—riding into battle without fear, challenging his foes to single combat, loyal to the death. A samurai would not stoop to spying, wearing a disguise, or killing in secret. But these things can be necessary in a time of war. And so they became the roles of ninjas, who also called themselves *shinobi* (SHIH-noh-bee).

It's likely that there were some female ninjas, sometimes called "deadly flowers." But few records survive of their names, training, or exploits. One exception, however, is Mochizuki Chiyome (or Chiyojo), who, according to legend, organized a secret cadre of female ninjas for the warlord Takeda Shingen during the 1500s. She is said to have taken in girls who were orphaned or abandoned in the chaos of the civil wars that raged through Japan in that century, trained them, and used them to gather information to serve Takeda's purposes.

For more information on female ninjas and Madame Chiyome, you might enjoy:

Uppity Women of Medieval Times by Vicki León

Ninja: The True Story of Japan's Secret Warrior Cult by Stephen Turnbull

Ninja Attack! True Tales of Assassins, Samurai, and Outlaws by Hiroko Yoda and Matt Alt

Ghosts and Demons

The folklore of Japan is full of *yurei* (ghosts) and *yokai* or *bakemono* (supernatural creatures, monsters, or demons). They range from merely spooky or mischievous to downright terrifying. Kata, Ichiro, and Saiko encounter some well-known creatures on their adventures, including:

Centipede: The centipede that attacks Kata in the kitchen might be a smaller relative of the enormous, multi-legged creature that was said to live under a mountain near Lake Biwa and prey on the children of dragons.

Double-mouthed woman, or *futakuchi onna:* (FOO-tah-KOO-chee OH-na): Most double-mouthed women are not as ferocious as Okui. One can usually pass for a perfectly ordinary person, even to her close friends and family, keeping the second mouth on the back of her head concealed under her hair. Her true nature shows only at night, when she sneaks into the kitchen and devours all the food she can find. However, she does not usually prey on her guests.

Fox: The Japanese red fox, or *kitsune* (KEY-tsoo-nay), is a clever trickster, and some are able to transform themselves into human beings (although they tend to keep the tail). They are powerful and unpredictable creatures. Some may play tricks on humans, some may kill, and some may be helpers or guides. White foxes are messengers of Inari, the god of rice, wealth, and the harvest.

Ghosts: Japanese folklore is rich in ghost stories. The spirits of those who were murdered or betrayed might come back as angry ghosts who inflict misfortune on the living. Hungry ghosts are spirits whose descendants do not take proper care of them by bringing prayers and offerings. They can strike their victims with illness or disease. Slain warriors haunt battlefields, and dead mothers sometimes return to be sure their children are well cared for. Not all ghosts are dangerous, but all can be identified by one clue: they have no feet.

Nue (NEW-ay): *Nue* are particularly hard to describe, because they often travel surrounded by a dense black cloud, and a single glimpse of them brings on serious illness. They seem to be some combination of monkey, tiger, snake, and possibly *tanuki* (Japanese raccoon), and are best avoided at all cost.

Tengu (TEN-goo): Half-crow and half-man, *tengu* are known for their skills with weapons. These tricksters and mischief-makers are sometimes said to cause plagues and other natural disasters. They tend to attack travelers who penetrate into their forest homes, but they have also been known to teach the martial arts to a few favored human disciples.

If you are interested in knowing more about Japanese monsters and demons, you might try *Yokai Attack! The Japanese Monster Survival Guide* by Hiroko Yoda and Matt Alt.